Girl Code

BROOKELYN MOSLEY

Cover Design by James, GoOnWrite.com

Join my BK Insiders Club to receive exclusive updates including sneak previews of chapters from new releases along with other Brookelyn Mosley news. You'll receive a complimentary short story just for signing up!

BrookelynMosley.com

Disclaimer

This is a work of fiction. Names, places, characters and events are all works of fiction for the reader's enjoyment. Any similarities to real people, places, events, living or dead are all a coincidence.

This story contains sexually explicit content that is intended for ADULTS ONLY (18 years or older)

Other Works By Brookelyn Mosley

Novellas

No Fraternizing, Pt. 1
No Fraternizing, Pt. 2
No Fraternizing, Pt. 3
Love, Hate & Revenge, Pt. 1
Love, Hate & Revenge, Pt. 2
Love, Hate & Revenge, Pt. 3
Forbidden: An Anthology
Mr. & Mrs. Jones

Short Stories

Just Friends
Lena's Ex-File
Chateau Luxure
Dream Boss
Unsilent Knight

Acknowledgements

I'd like to take the time out to thank all those who believed in me before I knew to believe in myself. Especially my husband who was my first official fan, other than myself. Thank you to all who have taken a chance on a new author, who just wants to write and create, by purchasing one of my novellas or short stories. You're all my loves and I appreciate your support more than words could ever describe. Thank you for your continued love. It's my inspiration, my soul food, and my fuel to keep creating.

Dedication

This is dedicated to all the lovers who started out as damn good friends.

"I love you and want to be with you until my final breath. Love you in this lifetime and then again in the next." - Amir Jones

Table Of
CONTENTS

Prologue

BROOKLYN, 2004

The sun had gone down hours before Melodee and Amir walked out to her backyard. They were headed to her tree house like they did on most nights after school.

"Ladies first," he said with a smile as he took her hand to help her step on the first wooden board nailed to the tree trunk.

She smiled back, allowing him to hold her hand for a second before slipping her hand free once she was securely on the second board.

The moment she reached the top, she flicked on her flashlight, shining the light through the tree house's entrance to see where she was stepping.

"You got the weed, right?" she asked as she ducked into the cramped house. Her father, Melvin, received three splinters and a sprained thumb when he built the tree house with his bare hands 10-years ago. She begged him to construct the little wooden house after she watched the children in several episodes of Barney climb in and out of their tree house. At fifteen and just 5'3, she could still fit comfortably through the door and below the ceiling.

"Yup," Amir answered. He lowered his head and hunched his shoulders on his six-foot frame to walk through the door. By his seventeenth birthday, he'd shoot up another three inches.

The wood planks below them squeaked with their movements, the house shaking a little when Amir dropped his backpack on the floor before leaning the neck of his acoustic guitar against one of the four walls of the tree house. Amir kneeled in front of his backpack to remove the Al Green vinyl album he kept in his bag. He carried the album around not so much for entertainment but to use as a prop for nights like these.

Swatting away spider webs, he walked toward Melodee, clearing his path to join her on the floor.

The fall evening was dark, but it wasn't late enough for the crickets to chirp. A faint glow from the moon above lit up the night's sky which they could see from the window of the tree house.

Amir leaned back against the same boarded wall as Melodee. He pulled up the bottom of his hoodie to take it off and the hem of his high school-branded basketball shirt slightly lifted with it. At fifteen, he'd grown into his looks that summer before their sophomore year. He spent a lot of his time with his father, Samir, when school was out. When Samir wasn't cooped up in his Philly townhouse spinning vinyl records, he practically lived at the gym. Because of this, Amir took up lifting weights. He didn't care for it, but he did his best to keep up with his dad while running on the treadmill and lifting heavy dumbbells because he realized that was the only time Samir spoke to him.

Melodee snuck a peek at the toned lines on his defined abs when his shirt hiked up.

She arched a brow acknowledging this was something new. If his body had always been like that, she would have noticed before tonight.

When she thought he'd caught her looking, she forced herself to look away.

"You're taking forever to roll, A.J. We don't have all night. I have to study."

"I have to study," he mocked. "Such a bookworm. Patience, Mel."

Reclining farther back, he pushed his hand into his jeans pocket and pulled out a tiny dime bag of Kush he stole from his father's house along with a cigar.

On the cover of the Al Green vinyl, he also took from his father's house, he broke up the weed, unrolled the paper from the cigar, and sprinkled the green onto the paper. He rolled, licked, and sealed it before holding it up in her view and asked, "You ready?"

"Is water wet?" She grinned.

Half-an-hour later, the two were still sitting arm-to-arm, passing the joint back and forth between them. They blew the smoke out of their mouths and noses watching as the smolder swirled around them in the tree house before wafting out the entrance and windows.

They were quiet, listening to the leaves scrape against the roof overhead.

After their high set in, Amir reached for his backpack and pulled out two bags of Doritos and a bottle of orange Fanta soda. He handed her, her bag of Doritos and they ate their chips like it was their last meal on earth. Every time they bit down on a chip and it crunched loudly, they'd laugh.

"You chew like a damn cow," she teased.

He threw a chip in his mouth, leaned in closer to her and bit down on the chip hard so the sound of it crunching could echo in her ear. She shoved him away playfully, and he poked her on her side.

The two had been friends for going on two years, befriending each other in their homeroom class on the first day of high school as freshmen. From the first day they met, Melodee felt comfortable with Amir. Around him, she never had to worry about her hair looking right or saying the right things. To her, that comfort was priceless. Though they had a lot in common, smoking weed was a thing they shared and that brought them even closer during those high school years.

"You wrote any new songs, yet," she asked as she craned her neck up to empty the crumbs of the Doritos left in the bag into her mouth before gesturing for his orange soda.

"Yup," he confirmed, opening his mouth wide and tilting the bottle to let the soda fall to the back of his tongue.

"No backwash," she teased.

"Never that," he replied, passing the bottle to her. "I wrote a song about you."

Melodee turned her head to him and swallowed the last of her chips. "Why would you do that?"

"You inspire me. You're my muse."

"Whatever that is," she replied. "Do I get paid for that... being your muse?"

He laughed. "I can pay you when I make it big."

She pressed her lips together and tilted her head. "I won't want your money then, A.J. I'll have my own, duh."

They were quiet again as he chewed his lip, debating in his mind about if he should say what he was about to say next.

"Can I ask you something?"

The tone of his voice dropped to a whisper low. It made her teenage body react in a way she often ignored whenever she was around him. "Um... okay. What's up?"

"What do you think about us taking this," he said, gesturing to himself then back to her, "to another level."

"What do you mean?"

He sighed. "Come on, you know what I mean."

She looked at him shaking her head. "And why would we do that? Things are cool between us as is. Why change it?"

"Because I'm feeling you, Mel... a lot. And not as a friend."

Melodee shifted in her seat and it made the tree house sway on the branches a little. She rubbed the back of her neck when she turned to him. He stared at her as if trying to hypnotize her, making it difficult for her to look away. Many thoughts surfaced in Melodee's mind but she couldn't focus long enough to express any of them.

He licked his lips and scooted closer to her, the wood plank below them squeaking. His hand was on the curve of her chin when he leaned in prepared to kiss her.

"Ain't this a... Melodee Sanaa Delon!" they heard her mother, Deedra, yell from below the tree house, interrupting Amir's flow. "Little girl… I know your narrow ass ain't up there smoking, again."

Melodee cupped her hand over her mouth and she and Amir tried to suppress their laugh.

"Amir, I know you're up there, too. Damn weed heads. Anita," she turned to yell toward the open door leading to the kitchen, "they're out here smoking, again."

"What? You lying!" Anita said from inside Deedra's kitchen.

"Mmm-hmm. You got your mama out here looking for your ass," Deedra added. "And y'all up there getting high. I swear to God, if y'all don't get y'all asses down here, when I come up there it ain't gon' be a pretty scene."

They scrambled. Amir picked up the now tiny piece that remained of their joint and flicked it out the window behind the tree house.

"Got my damn backyard smelling like a Bob Marley concert. Y'all ain't moving fast enough. Get y'all asses down here quick."

"Come on," Melodee said through giggles as she moved toward the exit.

"Mel," Amir said. He grabbed his backpack and guitar and walked up to her. "I'm being real about what I said."

She glanced up into his eyes. When the moment was way too serious for her she lightened the mood by cracking a smile.

"A.J., that weed got you trippin' again, huh?" she teased. Melodee playfully punched him on his shoulder, "stop playing and let's go before this woman climb up here, for real."

A ghost of a frown tried to pull his lips down but Amir forced himself to smile back instead as he followed her out.

Chapter One

BROOKLYN, 2016

"Ugh, come on! Go already." Melodee sighed heavy for the fifth time behind the wheel of her cream white Audi as she sat in traffic on the Brooklyn Bridge.

The day reflected her attitude as dark clouds moved along the pale blue sky. She hoped for sun just like she hoped she'd wake up from the nightmare of that day. Melodee was on her way to her lawyer's office on an early and cloudy Monday morning to meet with her soon to be ex-husband and his lawyer to sign divorce papers.

Her eyes were two hours away from being bloodshot red after she spent her night crying tears into her pillow. She could barely pull herself together that morning to pull on her black blazer and matching pencil skirt to leave her condo to arrive to the meeting on time. On most days, she'd hit the snooze button on her phone's alarm clock due to her being tired from studying all night. Today, that snooze button was her crutch, put to work to help her avoid getting up and facing the day.

After two years of marriage, her husband Jaden served her with divorce papers. Three months before that, they celebrated their second anniversary. Suffice it to say, the decision to go through with the divorce shocked Melodee. But it was a must for Jaden. He wanted children, and she wanted a degree. At 27, Melodee was a year away from earning her PhD in clinical psychology. She had plans to open her own practice and counsel couples and families as a marriage and family therapist as well as teach in an accredited university. Jaden had just celebrated his 30th birthday in March and had baby fever after attending one too many baby showers and being the last of his friends to become a daddy.

"I don't want to be too old when I have kids. I want to have the energy to keep up with them," he'd tell her in one of their arguments over whether they should change their extra bedroom in their condo into a study or nursery.

But Melodee wasn't ready to be a mother. She wasn't sure if that was even a route in life she wanted to take, ever. What she was sure of was that her goal to be a certified psychologist was in her cards.

Besides, having her own practice and working for herself made her blush more than the thought of motherhood.

"Good morning Tri-state area. This is your girl, LaLa, and you are now tuned in to Power 102.4 with LaLa in the morning," the radio host's voice whispered through Melodee's radio that was turned down low. "I've got some new music from Amir Jones off his highly anticipated new album, Black Rose."

Amir's name was all Melodee needed to hear to perk right up in her seat. She stretched her arm forward to turn the volume on her car radio as high as the dial would allow.

"It's called 'Paper Thorns' and it's a banger!" the host added before playing the song.

The moment the bass in the song banged, Melodee nodded her head in time with the beat. Her boy, Amir Jones', voice rode the melody like a surfer on a wave, painting vivid pictures with just his words like he did with all of his hits. His vocals seeped out the speakers in Melodee's car and floated in then out of Melodee's ears, wrapping around her like a warm hug.

Melodee smiled big as her fingers around the steering wheel tapped along to the rhythm of his song's chorus.

His voice was smooth with vintage undertones. His sound effortless. Amir could sing the alphabets and it would be a hit. The critics couldn't stop comparing his voice to Al Green when Amir first came on to the music scene. They swore Amir's voice was like a new age version of the legendary singer's.

Her heart swelled with excitement over seeing her childhood homie in concert the Friday after Christmas with her best friend Sheena, who was also his ex-girlfriend.

The three of them along with Amir's best friend Anthony, were like the three musketeers, plus one, back in the day. With Sheena as

Amir's girl and Amir as Melodee's best guy friend, the three were always together. And because Melodee wasn't checking for anyone who wasn't a composition notebook or pencil, she was happy to be the third wheel.

Even back then, Amir was driven and in love with singing. He'd hum and sing the lyrics to classic R&B songs as he strolled down the halls of their Brooklyn high school, sometimes with his guitar strapped to his back. Though his talent was evident, no one imagined one day he'd grow up to be one of the hottest R&B artists in the world.

After school on Wednesdays and Fridays he'd hop on the number 5 train and take his vocals and his guitar across town to Harlem. There, he'd sit on a parked car in front of the brownstone of Dope Records' A&R, Raheem Dubois. For hours, Amir would sing whatever song that came to mind with the help of his guitar. And he'd sing the lyrics loud enough for the whole block to get an earful of his voice.

Those were the only two days Raheem worked from home, info Amir received from the receptionist at Dope Records after she found him camped out in front of the label's main office singing his heart out every day for a month.

One day while sitting outside of Raheem's home, Amir accidentally dropped his Yankee fitted on the sidewalk while strumming his guitar. He refused to stop strumming and singing and left the hat on the ground. People were so impressed with his voice they filled his cap with singles, fives, and even twenties as they passed him.

That same day, after singing in front of Raheem's home for two months straight, Raheem finally noticed Amir. More to the point, he noticed the mounds of cash spilling out of Amir's hat. Raheem suggested Amir visit Dope Records so the other execs could listen to him sing.

One month before Melodee, Sheena, and Amir's high school graduation, Amir got his record deal. That same day he also learned Sheena was pregnant.

"That was the new joint 'Paper Thorns' from R&B's prince of soul Amir Jones," host LaLa's voice boomed out of Melodee's loud radio and invaded the car once again. "His new album Black Rose is rumored to drop later this year. In other news, your boy is leading the pack in the upcoming Grammy awards ceremony. It was announced last night that Mr. Jones received eight Grammy nominations for his platinum LP All Night Stand, including album of the year! So, big shout out to him for doing the damn thing. Call me now at 800-555-5455 and let me know what your favorite song is off Amir Jones' Grammy-nominated album All Night Stand."

Melodee gasped at the news. She clapped her hands and did a little dance in her seat like she herself had received those nominations.

An hour later, and late to her meeting, she was a block away from her lawyer's office when the first drops of rain fell from the sky. Her smile turned down into a frown as she pulled into the parking lot of her lawyer's office building.

She fixed the lapel of her black blazer and checked her makeup in her rearview mirror, preparing herself to face the end and the forced beginning of her new life.

Chapter Two

White paper with black words. That's what the legal documents and all the legal jargon typed on them looked like to Melodee. For the past hour, she listened as her lawyer and Jaden's lawyer went back and forth about the items that would be divided between the estranged husband and wife. What she would keep and what he was taking with him. They were speaking as if the two were not sitting right there.

They all sat in a conference room and across from each other with a long steel table keeping them apart. Glass doors and tall windows added the finishes to the very gray room. This wasn't a room where love was made. It was where it came to die.

A sea of high-rises, that enclosed the office building they sat in, obstructed their view of anything pleasant. Loud pellets of water slapped against then slid down the tall glass windows as the rain continued falling from dark clouds.

Every time Melodee looked up to meet her eyes with Jaden's, he'd move his away.

They hadn't spoken a single word to one another since she arrived late. Even as their lives veered in opposite directions, Melodee's heart still beat with love for him. His wide shoulders that held up his slim neck were slouching the entire time he sat across from her. His eyes purposely preoccupied with either the papers in front of him or the blank space of wall behind Melodee.

She twisted her diamond wedding band around her ring finger using her thumb, wanting him to at least look at her once. To give her a reason not to sign her name on the line on the paper in front of her. She wanted him to tell her that they should stop all of this and resume being Mr. and Mrs. Roberts. Be in love the way they were two years earlier.

He did nothing of the sort. Jaden sat there silent only speaking when asked to by his lawyer.

The air was cold around him. And it wasn't because it was the first week of December. He was distant and had the attitude of someone who just wanted to get this over with and leave.

"We need to discuss alimony," Melodee's lawyer, Rhonda, said as she flipped through her stack of papers.

"I told you... I don't want his money, Rhonda," Melodee said in a low voice as her gaze dropped to her lap.

That's what everyone thought she wanted when she and Jaden were dating. Melodee's father worked for the city as a sanitation worker and her mother was a homemaker. Jaden's parents were the CEOs of a lucrative real estate company that owned two prominent buildings in the city. They started their company in the 1980s, selling shares of it in 2000 for over 2 million. With that money, they invested in other businesses like franchise laundromats, independent publishing companies, and three grocery stores. So, Jaden was paid before getting his degree in finance.

Jaden proposed to Melodee after dating for a year and before he brought her home to meet his parents. They'd met in a coffee shop while Jaden was on break from work at his accounting firm and Melodee was grabbing a cup of coffee before heading to one of her classes. After he introduced Melodee to his parents for the first time, his father adored her while his mother told him privately to get a Prenuptial Agreement.

Jaden didn't listen because he like Melodee believed they'd be together forever. And she told him the moment he got down on one knee and asked her to marry him on a beach in Tanzania that she was in love with him and not his money.

"Wait, what?" Rhonda said to Melodee. Rhonda leaned over the armrest of her chair and in Melodee's direction then whispered in her ear, "We've discussed this already and we decided it would be best for you to get a monthly stipend considering you're still a student. You don't earn enough to support the lifestyle he's set up for you."

Melodee repeated, "I don't want his money. Not a single penny of it."

Melodee peered over at Jaden who'd finally allowed his eyes to meet hers.

"I don't want or care about your money. You know I never did."

He scanned her face, and she did his, the two sitting in silence and holding their stares as their lawyers tried to make sense of Melodee's comment. Through the sounds of pens scribbling and papers rustling, Melodee maintained eye contact with Jaden until he released an uneven sigh then looked away, resuming his stare elsewhere.

Melodee exhaled loudly. "All I ask is that I keep the condo and my car."

"Fine, whatever," Jaden replied not missing a beat. Those were the only words spoken to each other during the entire meeting.

When the meeting was over and the papers were signed making Jaden and Melodee officially divorcees, Jaden was out of there faster than a track runner.

No bye. No have a nice life. Nothing. It was as if they weren't once in love. Like they never made love. As if Melodee was just a blip in his past, nothing more.

She sat in her car in the parking lot of the building crying into her hands, the tears smearing her makeup, mascara rolling down her cheeks dripping salty black tears onto her white dress shirt.

The thought of returning home alone and sleeping in their custom yet empty king-sized bed, weighed heavy on her heart. She recalled the day they moved into their condo. The bare white walls were the backdrop to the love they made, the kitchen counter their makeshift mattress. Their moans the soundtrack to their first night. Her mind wandered to the little memories he left behind that she'd need to trash the moment she walked through the doors.

Things like the letter he wrote the night before their wedding and presented to her during their honeymoon. In the letter, he promised her a life fit for a queen because she deserved that and more. She kept the handwritten letter in an ivory white picture frame and sat it on her vanity table so she could see it every morning. There was also their handwritten vows they framed and sat atop their fireplace mantle. Vows he wrote assuring her that rough days would be sanded with patience and understanding because love is a verb and marriage takes work.

She cried until the tears could no longer pool in her eyes. And when she could cry no more, she drove home to her empty condo that was now a reminder of what she no longer had, a husband.

Chapter Three

Music banged out of the floor and overhead speakers like a jackhammer and vibrated past patrons at the bar, through well-dressed men and women grinding on the dance floor, and out Club Déjà Vu's doors. A long line of wannabe club attendees stood outside, vying for the attention of the hostess so she'd grant them access. This was no ordinary Friday night party, it was the after-party for Grammy nominated singer Amir Jones and Grammy award-winning MC, Abacus. The people in line either came directly from Amir and Abacus' joint sold out concert at Madison Square Garden or from their homes following hours of primping themselves in their mirrors.

It was the day after Christmas. Ornaments and Christmas lights hung from store windows while day-old pies still sugared the air.

Melodee and Sheena's heels clicked and clacked against the city's sidewalk as they made their way past the snake line of shivering clubbers headed straight to Club Déjà Vu's front doors. Sheena's husband Ray was an executive at a high-end black car company in

New York City and had extra tickets to Amir and Abacus' concert after the company's Christmas giveaway. Ray was aware of how much his wife adored Abacus. She played his music loud and proud at home and in her car, so Ray didn't hesitate to cop her two tickets to Abacus' concert along with getting her name put on the guest list for the after-party.

Sheena had already told Ray about her and Amir's past, but he wasn't worried. Ray was confident Sheena understood where home was. Plus, Sheena absolutely hated Amir, anyway.

Continuing up the path of the sidewalk, Melodee scanned the bodies of people waiting in line. The women wore dresses that hugged their curves so tight, the seams of their garments pulled at the sides. Their breasts were perked up so high, the mounds practically grazed their jawlines. Their heels were like skyscrapers with some of their bare toes hanging out and over the mouth of their shoes.

The men went all out too. Designer shirts, slacks, and shoes. They finished their looks with designer shades they kept over their eyes even though it was two hours till midnight. It was like a standard checklist was passed around before that night to make sure everyone wore their Club Déjà Vu uniforms.

Sheena pulled at Melodee's hand. "Come on girl, we're already on the list."

At the suggestion of her friend, Melodee picked up a new outfit for the night- a long-sleeved pink sequined backless romper with a plunging V-neck that showed off her toned legs. The moment she saw the sequined romper, she had to get it since it was in her favorite color, pink. On her feet were silver metallic strappy heels she insisted on being lower than four inches since her common sense told her dancing and then walking in anything higher would be muscle suicide. She kept warm in a black asymmetrical wool coat that stopped at her knees.

They walked to the front of the line and a tall thin leggy brunette with a clipboard asked for their names. Sheena gave her the info and when the hostess found them on the list, she checked them off then gave a head nod to the bald bulky bouncer with shoulders so wide, he looked like he had to turn sideways to walk through doors. He unclipped a red velvet rope and gestured for the ladies to walk through to enter.

Sheena's grin could not be contained as she glanced over her shoulder at Melodee then grabbed her hand to enter the club. There were hordes of paparazzi posted up on one side of the club's foyer near the entrance. Opposite the photogs, was a red carpet and backdrop with the club's logo, Amir and Abacus' names, and a few liquor sponsors printed all over. With camera in hand, they snapped pictures of Sheena and Melodee as they walked the carpet. Sheena stopped for a moment to strike a pose and Melodee stood there looking at her.

"Smile, beautiful," one photographer said to Melodee.

She shook her head but couldn't stop the curve of a smile pulling at her lips. Melodee was a self-assured woman normally. However, as a recent divorcee, hearing a man call her beautiful brightened her spirits a little.

"Are you two Deja Models?" another photographer asked.

Before Sheena could part her lips to respond, Melodee chimed in. "We're nobodies," grabbing Sheena by the hand and pulling her out of her pose and off the red carpet.

"Girl, why would you say that? I don't know about us being nobodies. We're damn near celebrities tonight being able to get in here. Did you see that line?"

Melodee kissed her teeth. "We are nobody important. We're not even Deja Models," she giggled. "Don't make them waste camera space on us basic chicks."

"Basic? Ha!" Sheena retorted, stopping in front of a large platinum-plated mirror to comb her fingers through her bottle-blonde natural curls. "Speak for yourself. I'm a superstar tonight, baby!"

The moment they stepped down the stairs and entered the main club area, Melodee's jaw dropped and her eyes stretched wide enough to see the whites of her eyes. The place was massive and brimming with people. All she could see were moving heads on the dance floor as the crowd danced to Abacus' single "Money & Moet." Deja Models swung either overhead on mounted swings, danced in bedazzled cages, or splashed each other playfully in tubs filled with silver glitter. Only thing to keep them warm were their platinum metallic bikini bottoms and pasties shaped like a pool of whip cream with a cherry on top. The room was dipped in platinum and white from the bar counter to the dance floor. The only thing with color was the DJ's booth that lit up with flashing neon lights.

Bottle service girls weaved through the crowds holding bottles over their heads. With sparklers crackling from the necks of the champagne bottles they carried, they walked their way up to the VIP area. Now the VIP area was more chilled than anywhere else in the club. In an elevated skybox, a small group of people sat on white cushioned chairs in this decked out room looking down at clubbers dancing. Female clubbers had three layers of makeup painted on their faces looking like they left a Vogue editorial shoot before arriving at the club. Melodee had already spotted three celebrities. Her heart raced. She was star struck.

"Damn!" Sheena said rubbing her palms together as she looked on with Melodee.

"My thoughts exactly," Melodee replied.

Sheena pulled Melodee through the crowd and headed straight to the bar. For the past hour, she'd been talking about eating the olives and peanuts more than getting a drink.

At the bar, Sheena ordered two rum and cokes and handed Melodee her tiny clear plastic cup filled with the liquor and soda mix.

Sheena took one sip then gagged.

"Does this taste funny to you?" she asked holding her cup in Melodee's view.

Melodee was too busy taking in the scene to respond. She leaned back on her elbow and sipped her drink slow. She cased the club, watching as women and men competed for each other's attentions and danced provocatively with total strangers.

A frown slowly pulled her lips down.

Melodee believed this part of life was over for her years ago. She never delved into the dating scene having met Jaden during her first year of her doctoral program. Before then, there were a few guys she'd hook up with, but not date. She didn't believe in having romantic relationships while in school so Jaden was her first real boyfriend before they got married. It had always been them together, so this was all new. Her eyes pointed up at the elevated VIP room, searching for a familiar face.

"Don't look so blue, boo," Sheena said loud so Melodee could hear her over the loud music. Sheena opted to sip on water, moving her hips to the beat of the song playing.

A guy walking past stepped into Melodee's view and when she focused on him, he smiled at her then licked his lips. Like the other brothers, he was wearing his club costume complete with sunglasses in an already dimmed room.

Melodee's lip turned up before she rolled her eyes. She spun around to face the bar.

"Is this what I have to look forward to?"

Sheena rubbed Melodee's back then pulled her into a side hug. "No. This is an exaggerated mess. Rule number one of dating is never date the guy you meet at the club. This is not where you're gonna find Mr. Right but you will find Mr. Right Now. Tonight, isn't about any of that, anyway. We're just here to clear our minds and let loose, right?"

Melodee forced a smile. "Right!"

An hour in and Melodee had finally gotten acclimated to her environment. She hadn't been to anything close to a club since getting married. Jaden was more of a homebody who preferred to spend his downtime at home in bed cuddled up watching TV. At home in bed was also more of Melodee's style, but when the time called for it and with the right amount of liquor, she could also be the life of the party. That part of her life, being a homebody, had been put to bed, but a new one was coming alive the longer she stayed and danced at Club Déjà Vu.

After they'd worked up a sweat on the dance floor moving their hips to Abacus and Amir's catalog of songs, Sheena and Melodee reconvened at the bar.

"I wonder if we'll see A.J. tonight," Melodee said to Sheena referring to Amir. "He was so good at The Garden, right?"

Sheena twisted her mouth. "I prefer we not see him. And he wasn't all that. His performance was aight, for what it was."

Melodee turned to face Sheena completely. "I'm sorry. The music must be too loud because I think you just lied and said the man was 'aight' when he brought the house down."

"Amir's music never did it for me, even when we were dating. The only reason he's gotten to this level in his career is because of those light brown eyes and that big sexy smile. His shirt is always off, so the ladies are more interested in his body than what he's singing about. He's a cute face and muscles but talent wise, meh," Sheena said, shrugging. She took a sip of her water and looked away.

"You're trippin'." Melodee laughed.

"So... what?" Sheena yelled over the music so Melodee could hear her. Unfortunately, half the bar including the bartenders could hear her, too. "You're an Amir groupie now?" she asked stepping back and crossing her arms.

"You know me better than that," Melodee replied taking a sip of the water she ordered.

"Well, the two of you were super tight back in the day and I would've never known him if you didn't know him first so I don't know. Whose bestie are you, again?"

"You know you're my girl and I always got your back. I was just asking a question, is all."

Sheena stared at her for a moment. Melodee stuck her tongue out at her, making a silly face. This made Sheena smile like a six-year-old on Christmas day. Sheena wrapped her arms around her best friend pulling her into a bear hug.

This was classic Sheena. She had the personality of Miami weather which was also the city she was born and raised. She could be bright and sunny one moment, dark and stormy the next, only to go back to being bright and sunny again at the snap of a finger. From the time they met and became friends their freshman years in high school, Melodee learned how to deal with her girlfriend better than anyone else, including Sheena's husband, Ray.

"I gotta pee," Melodee announced. "You want to come with me to the bathroom?"

"You go; I'll be here snacking on these olives. They're almost done and I'm still hungry!"

Typical of a female bathroom anywhere but especially at the club, the line was out the door. Melodee scowled when she got on at the back. Close to five-minutes later, she finally walked into a free stall to handle her business. Inside, she couldn't help but to notice how the voices tapered off, and the bathroom fell silent. She finished and stepped out of the stall, soaped and rinsed her hands under the water in the sink, and glanced from her left to her right trying to make sense of why the bathroom was empty now after being full minutes ago.

Even as she dried her hands under the hand dryer no one had yet to enter since she stepped out of the stall. Taking advantage of the free space and time, she stood in front of the full-length mirror and combed her fingers through her bra strap length curls, reapplied her MAC pink lip gloss to her full lips, and examined her face to make sure her tinted moisturizer was holding up to the heat in the club. She also checked to make sure her two pink diamond studs were still securely clasped to her earlobes. More than them being pretty, they were her insurance plan.

She checked herself out once more, admiring how she looked in her romper that sparkled under the bathroom's lights. Jaden would have never let her wear something like this out of the house. So, having it on at the club was empowering. She held her chin high and gave a nod of approval to herself in the mirror before turning to step out of the bathroom.

When she pulled open the door and glanced down the hall to her left, she scratched her head and grimaced. It was empty when just minutes ago there was a long line of women. The only person visible was a big and tall guy with high shoulders dressed in all black standing at the end of the hall that led back to the dance floor of the club. She could only see the back of his head because his body faced the dance floor.

What happened to the line? she thought to herself.

"Hey, stranger," he said over her right shoulder.

She turned in that direction and gasped, bringing her hand up to her mouth. Her fingers were barely able to conceal her bigger than life smile.

He was leaning against the wall not far from where she stood with his hands buried inside his pockets. Dressed in a white dress shirt, sleeves rolled up, with a black vest and matching tailored dress pants. His leather loafers were polished so well that the glint of light from the mini-chandelier overhead danced on the surface of his shoes. That same light gave even more life to his golden-brown complexion. The natural sheen in his pretty boy goatee sparkled and his light brown eyes twinkled when he looked at her. He flashed her his signature sexy smile, a smile that helped him land a multi-million-dollar toothpaste deal earlier that year.

She felt her knees get weak.

The wind pocket in the hallway drifted between them bringing the decadent scent of his Tom Ford cologne to where she stood, wafting it up her nose.

It was Amir Jones - superstar R&B singer who the media referred to as the prince of soul and who dubbed him The Sexiest Man Alive one month before. But to Melodee, he was just her childhood homie, her best guy friend from high school, and Sheena's first love.

Against the opposite wall was his best friend, Anthony, but everyone called him Big Ant. As his name implied, he was a big dude. Large like the bathroom doorway where Melodee stood. And because of that, Amir didn't hesitate to appoint him the head of his security. Melodee put two and two together and figured the bulky dude at the other end of the hall was a part of Amir's security team.

"Oh my God!" Melodee squealed walking up to Amir who met her halfway for a hug. The two embraced each other pulling one another close. Melodee wrapped her arms around the back of Amir's neck, her hands pressed flat against his strong back. His back was firm, muscles tight, and the feel of his body pressed against hers made her tingle. When his hand drifted down her exposed lower back she gently pulled away. The soft skin on her nipples stiffened, and she took a deep breath to calm them.

Her eyes traveled down the length of Amir's body. He'd always been a good-looking brother. But as *the* Amir Jones, he was the total package. He embodied the dangerous combination of sexy - height, body, and suaveness. A triple threat. Melodee mentally kicked herself for feeling like a heart-eyed emoji.

"What's up, A.J.?" she asked.

He tapped his hand against his chest and fanned out his fingers on his chest bone. "Wow, I haven't been called that in a while."

Melodee gasped. "Oh, is it still cool for me to call you that?"

"Absolutely!" he replied with no hesitation. "That just took me back. No one has called me that since..." he paused. "The only other person who called me that was mama."

Melodee's smile turned down into a frown and her eyes watered. Her heart grew heavy with thoughts of when she first learned Amir's mother, Anita Jones, lost her battle with breast cancer that January. She wanted so bad to attend the funeral, to pay her respects, but Amir made the funeral service private and closed to the public. If you didn't receive an invitation, you weren't allowed within 300-feet of the service.

"I'm so sorry about Ms. Anita. You know I loved your mama... like for real, for real."

Amir inhaled the air around him then ran his hand over his curly top fade before releasing an uneven sigh through his nose. It was clear he was still grieving. "I know, she loved you, too."

Big Ant still standing on the opposite wall cleared his throat then waved his hands in the air to get her attention. "Um, hi?"

Melodee and Amir broke out laughing and this lightened the mood.

"Hey Ant!" Melodee said giving Anthony a hug, her arms barely able to reach even halfway around him.

Ant said, "Look at you looking good and shit. Got your thighs all out and oiled in this cold."

She swatted him with her hand. "Shut up."

Melodee, Anthony, Amir and Sheena were tight as thieves back when they were teenagers. They spent a lot of their times together once Amir and Sheena dated. They ended up drifting apart after graduation, but Melodee maintained her tight friendship with Sheena and Amir and Big Ant's bond remained iron strong.

Amir, Melodee, and Anthony caught each other up on what was new in their lives. Mostly Melodee and Anthony had stuff to share since anything relevant in Amir's personal life was constantly plastered on the pages of tabloids.

"You cleared out this hall for me?"

Amir nodded.

"Where'd they go? Because those ladies looked like they'd sell their first born for a stall to pee."

"VIP. They'll hold it in just to rub shoulders with celebrities," Amir replied.

Big Ant said, "So what's up? I saw you were here with Sheena."

"How you saw that?"

"From VIP," Amir mumbled.

"Oh ok. Yeah, she's at the bar right now if you—"

"We're about to head out," Amir interjected.

As Ant spoke again, Amir tasked himself with taking in a final view of Melodee's curves, for now. And even after she caught him staring and checking her out he kept at it finding it impossible to break his stare.

Melodee's cheeks grew warm from blushing at Amir who hadn't stopped undressing her with his eyes. This was a look she wasn't used to getting from him as compared to when they were in high school.

He was bolder and more deliberate with his gawk. She couldn't deny it; he was turning her on.

Her stomach fluttered and her breathing quickened every time their eyes stayed on each other for longer than five seconds. And she had to force herself not to smile at him because she worried that if he smiled back, she'd faint.

"I'm having a little something at my Tribeca loft," Amir added.

Melodee arched a brow then said, "Well, excuse me!"

He laughed. "I want you and Sheena to come through. It could be like old times; But better." He popped his collar.

Melodee snickered before looking over her shoulder toward the bar. She already knew Sheena wouldn't be with it, but she would not tell him that.

"Um... I'll check with her. If she's down, then we'll be there."

Amir released a deep, weighted sigh. "Aight. But do a good job convincing her, I remember how stubborn she can be. I really want to see you... I mean y'all, there tonight, aight?"

"Aight." Melodee nodded.

By the bar, Sheena was still stuffing her mouth with briny green olives when Melodee walked up beside her.

"Damn, took you long enough. They were giving away freebies in there, or something?" Sheena asked, parts of the olive flying out of her mouth when she spoke.

"Or something," Melodee replied. "Guess who I bumped into?"

Sheena gasped then gave Melodee her full attention. "Beyoncé?! I thought I saw her."

"No, someone better. Amir!"

Sheena stopped chewing her olives for a moment. "First, no one is better than Beyoncé, OK? Secondly... Oh." She scowled.

"Okay, well, he invited us to his loft in Tribeca to his after, after-party." Melodee moved her hips to the beat of the song playing, bumping her hip with Sheena to get her amped.

"Oh?"

"You wanna go?"

"No."

"Why not?"

Sheena rolled her eyes and went right back to eating the olives. The female bartender with long Senegalese twists watched Sheena from the side of her eye, annoyed that she would need to refill the olives container for the third time that night. The glare Sheena shot her when she noticed she was staring let the bartender know not to even bother saying anything about it, or else.

"You know why," Sheena replied.

"But that happened ten years ago, can't you forgive?"

"Not when I still can't have a baby." Sheena's eyes watered, and she dropped the olive she was about to put in her mouth into her cup of water.

Melodee inhaled the warm club air through her nose and blew it out through her mouth

"You go," Sheena insisted after their moment of silence.

"What, no! I can't do that to you."

"It's cool. I want you to go." Sheena looped her arm with her best friend's and rested her head on her shoulder. Her curly blonde coils tickled the bottom of Melodee's chin. "Maybe you can find a nice distraction at the party who will help you forget all about how fucked up your month's been."

Melodee thought about it for a moment. "You're sure you're fine with me going? For real, for real?"

"Yes, I insist. I'm gonna go home to my husband so we can work on baby making. Nothing may not be happening but at least the practice is epic." Sheena smiled coyly.

Melodee considered the thought, then said, "Okay!"

As they turned on their heels to exit the club, Sheena said to Melodee, "But you gotta promise me one thing."

"What's that?"

"You tell me all that happened at that party. I want all the details, from the people who were there to the way his place looked. You know I'm nosy like that."

Melodee glanced over at her friend and smiled from ear-to-ear, then stuck out her pinky for Sheena to loop with hers. "Promise."

Chapter Four

The cab Melodee flagged down in front of the club and rode in across town, stopped in front of a building on Hudson Street in Manhattan that resembled a warehouse. She paid the driver before pushing open the car door to step out. Standing on the curb as he drove off, her head tilted back as she took in the height of the building. It was so high, if she didn't know any better she'd believe the roof disappeared into the night's sky.

She approached the heavy glass lobby door and a black-suited gentleman greeted her before she could even enter. She told him exactly what Big Ant told her to say when Ant gave her the address to the loft.

"I'm here for Mr. Jones' soiree."

The doorman showed her to the elevator and pressed the top floor for her. There was only one door on the floor once she stepped off the elevator. Before she could knock on it, Big Ant slid the heavy metal door open.

"Thank you," he praised, pressing his chubby palms together like he would say a prayer if given the chance. "Now he can stop asking me every 10-minutes if you arrived yet."

Melodee giggled while walking inside.

"Where's Sheena?"

"Now you know we would've had a better chance of getting a cat to play piano than getting Sheena to come here. I'm her best friend, not a magician."

"Dang! She's still mad at him?" Big Ant replied, sliding the loft door closed.

Melodee probably would have been able to reply if her jaw wasn't so far from her upper lip as it hung open in awe of the loft.

Amir's loft was as enormous as a football field with a high 12-inch ceiling held up by imported roman-style columns. She marveled at the custom-made chandelier sculpted from hand-blown glass, then at the oversized windows wedged between the exposed brick walls. A wall-sized original Basquiat painting hung near the bottom of his glass staircase that lead the way to one of his bedrooms. The place was full of people, a lot of them looking like some of the clubbers from Déjà Vu. Most of them were women who had weaves down their backs, professionally done makeup, and their looks finished off with perfect outfits and the accessories to boot.

"Damn," Melodee whispered to herself.

"It's dope, right?" Big Ant asked looking around the place like he was seeing it for the first time. "A," he said referring to Amir, "wants to sell. He feels it's too much space for just him."

"He's crazy," she replied still glancing over the loft. "Where is he, anyway?"

"He's on a business call, but he'll be out in a few minutes. You're all right alone? I gotta go watch the door. Can't let just anybody in, you know?"

Melodee smiled. "Yeah, I'm good, Mr. Security."

She stepped into the kitchen where the bottles of champagne chilled in ice filled buckets that sat on a black granite counter.

While she poured herself a glass, two men dressed in tailored two-piece suits walked in bursting with laughter and conversation.

"I hope he plays that album tonight."

"Yeah, me too, I can't stop playing Paper Thorns and if the rumors are true, every song on Black Rose is single worthy."

"They say Black Rose is his best album to date, and that's saying a lot since his last one was incredible. The only people who've listened to Black Rose are the label executives."

"I'm so jealous!"

"I also heard he's refusing to send review copies to critics."

"Seriously?"

"Won't even announce an official release date. I think he's up to something."

She left them in the kitchen still talking and walked into the living room to have a seat on the long cream-colored couch that was already occupied by two other ladies. In front of her, on the flat screen that was encased in walnut-colored panels, played his new video for "Paper Thorns." In it, Amir sang on a rooftop in an exotic location with nothing on but a pair of jeans. Melodee snorted to herself when she remembered Sheena saying that he never had his shirt on.

It was going on half-an-hour since she arrived and still there was no Amir. So, Melodee pulled out her phone from her silver clutch. She tapped into her Facebook app and scrolled through her timeline. Melodee hardly posted photos or status updates, but she loved keeping up with friends and family who shared just about everything on social media. She took a sip of her champagne and nearly choked on the bubbly drink when she gasped at what she saw.

A photo of Jaden caught her eye. It was of him and his new girl holding a sonogram while he kissed her on her cheek. Melodee's heart sank when she read the caption where he revealed they were also planning to get married. The photo left her dazed. Her posture stiffened as she kept rereading the caption. She knew she should have listened to Sheena when she told her to unfriend him. Get rid of him in real life and online.

"Ohhh! They are goals," said the girl sitting to Melodee's right with her gaze down on Melodee's phone. "Is that your homegirl and her man?"

Her friend leaned forward beside her, also curious.

Melodee closed out her phone and pulled air through her nose to stop the tears from forming in her eyes.

"Oops, I don't think that's the homegirl, but that might be her man," the other girl said.

Both women were video girl beautiful with perfectly coifed weaves, long false lashes to complement their beat faces. Their bodies, even as they sat beside Melodee, defied the laws of physics.

"My ex-husband," Melodee mumbled before downing her half full glass of champagne.

"Well, you're cuter than her anyway so he downgraded. I'm Micha and this is Samia."

Melodee forced herself to smile back. "Melodee."

"Your earrings are so cute! Are those pink diamonds?!" Samia asked.

"Yeah."

"Real?" Micha asked leaning in closer to Melodee to get a better look.

"Yup."

Melodee clenched her jaw at the irony of the moment. The earrings were a gift from her ex-husband, given to her on their wedding day. Normally, Melodee kept them locked away in her jewelry box but wore them that night because it was the only jewelry that was real and matched her outfit. She used to wear them casually to run errands or go to the gym, but now on her own, they were her insurance plan in case she needed to quit her receptionist job to focus full-time on school.

Samia leaned over her friend to tap Melodee on the knee. "Which rapper gave you those? It was Abacus, huh? I knew I recognized you! You were in his video for "Money & Moet," right? You were the girl with the green booty shorts who twerked on that money green Jaguar."

Melodee furrowed her brows shaking her head. "That wasn't me."

"Oh, so you're a make-up artist?" Samia asked.

"No."

"Stylist?" Micha asked next.

"Uh-uh."

"So what do you do?"

Melodee scratched the back of her head then smiled. "I'm just a student at NYU. I'm a year away from getting my PhD in clinical psychology, though!" Just saying it made her heart beat with happiness and brightened her mood. Those long nights of studying and sacrificing her time and energy would soon pay off when she marched across that stage in her cap and gown to get her doctorate.

Micha and Samia were silent for a moment, staring at Melodee.

"Oh," Micha said, wrinkling her nose as she leaned back with folded arms. "She's one of those college girls."

Samia was silent for a moment before deciding to keep probing with questions. "Well, how did you get in here?"

Melodee frowned but then brushed off their disinterest in her accomplishment. "Amir and I were friends in high school."

Micha perked right back up in her seat. "Oh okay! Girl, why you ain't just say that! So, you know him?"

"Yeah, he used to be my best friend's boyfriend."

Micha and Samia flashed each other a look then turned their attention back on Melodee.

"And she was okay with you coming here?!" Samia asked.

"Yeah... why?

"Girl code!" Micha and Samia said at the same time.

Melodee stared at them confused.

"If I'm through with a guy, all my girls are too," Micha added.

Samia nodded. "Meaning, if we break up you might as well be dead to me and my friends. They walk right past your ass when they see you, no exceptions. No hi, bye, nothing. Unless we back on in which case it's all good again."

Melodee shook her head. "That's not how it is with me and my homegirl. She insisted that I come tonight."

"And you believed her?" Micha asked before bursting into a fit of giggles. "You better hope she takes your call in the morning."

Melodee sat back and bit her lip in thought.

"Look, forget about all that right now," Samia suggested. "Since you're not here for self, hook us up with your boy."

"Who?"

"Amir!" Samia and Micha said at the same time.

"The both of you?"

They nodded. Melodee's eyes bounced from Micha to Samia. "And sleeping with the same guy isn't breaking the rule of girl code?"

"Not when you have an understanding," Micha explained.

"Plus, I hear Amir prefers two at a time, anyway," Samia said licking her lips.

"Threesomes?" Melodee inquired. Her back was now off the couch, her ears wide open.

Both Samia and Micha nodded, biting their lips with sex in their eyes.

Samia leaned in, gesturing for Melodee to move in closer so she could speak low enough for only them three to hear. "This girl I met at a video shoot I did about a month ago said that he has a huge sexual appetite and that one girl just ain't enough. She said he is so giving that when you're sharing with the other girl, you still get more than enough from him. But if you're the only one fucking him, you'll tire out because he takes forever to come. You would have gotten yours twice, and he still hasn't busted yet."

Melodee's jaw dropped. "Really?"

Micha's right brow arched, and she peered at Melodee from the side of her eye. "You're not getting curious... are you?"

Samia and Micha stared at Melodee. The tip of Melodee's tongue pressed against the roof of her mouth and she fixed her lips to tell them no.

"Ayo, Mel!" Amir called for Melodee over her shoulder.

She turned to see him approaching behind her, shaking hands with the guys and giving kisses on the cheeks to some of the ladies along the way.

"Y'all are too much." Melodee collected her clutch and stood to her feet.

"Hold up." Micha gently grabbed her hand. "Don't forget to hook us up, girl." She winked.

"Don't worry. I got you." Melodee smiled.

She met up with Amir at the far end of the room and he pulled her into a hug. When he released her, he smiled big and her heart melted. Right then she questioned if it was smart for her to be there with him if he made her feel like that.

"You came."

"Of course."

His eyes were going to work again on her breasts, hips, and bare legs.

She punched him on the arm.

"Stop that."

"Stop what?" he asked, wetting his lips with his tongue.

Melodee fought back her smile.

"Let's go out on the terrace," he said pulling her along.

"Terrace? It's cold as hell outside."

"Don't worry, you won't be cold."

"Oh wait. Um… those two ladies," she said, pointing at Micha and Samia who were now turned in their seats looking back at Melodee and Amir smiling and waving. "They said they're down for whatever if you are."

Amir looked down at Melodee who was about ten inches shorter than him then back over toward where she pointed. He gave Micha and Samia a head nod and smiled politely.

"I'll pass. Come on," he said grabbing Melodee's hand and guiding her to the terrace.

Chapter Five

Amir's terrace looked like a mini-park, complete with pruned bushes, a small flower garden, and a tree. Tucked in the corner next to the door leading to one of his three bedrooms was a small koi pond with two orange and gold koi fish. He had a cabana-like lounge chair that swung on sturdy gold chains and took up one side of the terrace. A couple of chairs and a table sat at the center of the terrace. In view was the Freedom Tower where the World Trade Center used to be. It stood so close, Melodee reached out her hands, knowing that she wouldn't be able to touch it, but trying anyway.

"Don't let anyone on the terrace while I'm out here, aight?" Amir said to one of his bodyguards.

The big bulky guy nodded, stepped back into the loft, pulling the door shut and locking it. The bright lights in the loft became a soft glow after Amir's bodyguard pulled the curtains closed on the other side.

"Are you kidding me with this?" she asked, pointing at the skyscraper. "This is amazing."

He shrugged his shoulders before sitting back in the swinging lounge chair. He kept the chair from swinging by planting his designer leather shoe on the edge of the coffee table in front of him.

Her eyes bounced from him to the skyscraper then back on him. "Do you know how blessed you are?"

"Blessed, maybe. Grateful, definitely."

Melodee waved him off as she walked over to where he sat and dropped herself down on the chair. She removed her wool coat and leaned forward to unstrap her shoes, her fingers moving gracefully over the chromed clasps as Amir watched her every move. She slipped them off, pulling her legs up on the lounge chair, folding them Indian style. Her head lolled over the back of the chair and she closed her eyes, taking a deep breath and exhaling into the night air.

There was a wood and glass terrace awning overhead. On the other side of the glass coffee table in front of them was a Brown Jordan's modular Equinox fireplace that burned coal, the fire blazing on top moving with the wind. Beside the swinging lounge chairs and curving high over them, were two heated lamps. With all the heating supplies keeping the cold out, the terrace felt like spring in December.

She opened her eyes and twisted her head in Amir's direction to find him staring at her.

"What?" she asked sitting up.

"Nothing. You just look like you're right at home."

She pursed her lips. "Whatever. So, why'd you pass up the opportunity to spend the night with the ménage twins?" She asked referring to Micha and Samia.

Amir scoffed. "I watched that show already and I'm tired of the repeats."

Melodee giggled. "You've had sex with them already?"

Amir replied by shaking his head. "Might as well have, they're all the same."

"You didn't have a problem with that back in the day, playboy. Sheena had the hardest time keeping your ass in check and your eyes facing forward and not on the next fat booty."

Amir waved her off. He brought his hands behind his head, leaning his elbow over the headrest with eyes facing forward. "Key phrase: back in the day. I was a boy then. Real men require a little more class and sophistication. At least the girls made me chase them a little. These women now don't make me do shit. They're willing to bust it open for a Celine bag or a selfie on Instagram." He turned to look at her. "Do you know a girl almost sucked my dick on stage in Houston? If I didn't tell her to get her ass up off the floor, she would have taken it to the head in front of thousands for no other reason besides getting her 15-minutes of fame."

Melodee looked over at him with her jaw slacked.

"Exactly my reaction," he said laughing loudly. "I'm at the stage in my life where I need a classic kind of attraction, you know? The brown Burberry trench coat with sexy lingerie under it, red heels, and lips painted red. Tease a brother a little. Let me get to experience the anticipation. I'll be the first guy to admit that it'll make me appreciate the booty more once I finally get it."

"Mmm-hmm," was all Melodee said.

They sat quietly for a moment, listening to the city sounds of honking cars and the winter wind blowing atop the terrace awning.

"Speaking of Sheena, what's up with her? Why she still mad at me?"

Melodee sighed and looked away. If she could avoid talking about Sheena's reasons for holding a grudge against Amir it would be for the best.

"You know how Sheena can be."

Amir was quiet for a moment, fiddling with his fingers. "So... what's new with her?"

Melodee unfolded her legs and turned to face him. "She's married now."

"Oh wow."

"And they're trying to have a baby but it's taking longer than expected. But… yeah." Melodee paused on purpose, making sure every word that left her lips was as simplistic as possible. The truth was Sheena and her husband Ray had been trying to conceive since that summer. She got pregnant two months prior to she and Ray's wedding but miscarried a month before they said, "I do." Since that time, they'd been trying but with no luck. Per the three doctors Sheena has met with, she may be unable to conceive or even carry a baby past her first trimester. They said the reason for this stems from the abortion Amir pressured her into having when they were in high school.

"Well, I'm happy for her. I wish she would have come tonight. It would have given us an opportunity to squash our beef," Amir replied.

Melodee wanted to say something but left well enough alone.

"And what about you? You got a husband at the crib waiting for you to come home?" He was looking her right in her eyes, searching for the answer before she could even reply.

She shook her head first then let the weight of her head hang over the back edge of the swinging lounge chair. "Not as of two weeks ago."

Amir remained silent.

"I signed divorce papers on the seventh of this month."

"Word? What happened?"

Though the heat lamps and concrete fireplace were canceling most of the cold air out on the terrace, a small breeze managed to brush past her neck making her shiver.

"He wanted a baby, I wanted a degree. Jaden wasn't willing to wait and I wasn't willing to settle. We argued everyday about it until one day he packed up his stuff and left." She sighed. "I came home literally the next day to find divorce papers on our kitchen counter along with his wedding band. That was two months ago."

"Damn, that fast?"

Melodee closed her eyes and tried to blink back her tears but that was useless. Whenever she cried, there was no point in holding it in because once she started she had to ride with her emotions. She let her tears slip from her eyes and felt them slide down the side of her cheeks. She patted them away with her fingers, keeping her eyes pointing up at the blank night sky. "He wouldn't even look at me at the meeting where we signed the papers. We sat in that conference room together and he wouldn't even make eye contact with me for longer than a second. How can someone who said they loved me with every fiber of their being just decide they don't want me anymore because of a baby who doesn't even exist? How is that possible? And the worst part is not that we're divorced, but that he moves lightning fast with change. He's already gotten another woman pregnant and announced he's getting married, again, before the ink on our fucking divorce papers dried."

"Wait, what?"

"Which means," Melodee continued, "He was already fucking this woman when I was under the impression that our marriage could be fixed if he'd just look at me. In his eyes, he was already a divorced man before he signed on that dotted line. Meanwhile, like an idiot, I was still wearing my wedding ring at the meeting, hoping he would notice it and see that I hadn't given up on us, not even in that moment."

She dropped her face into her hands. "Because of him switching shit up, I had to take a shitty ass receptionist job with Dr. Sherida Pierce, a.k.a Dr. Pain In My Fucking Ass." She grunted. "I thought I had it all figured out when we got married. I was so wrong. All I have left to show for our marriage is my condo, my car, and these earrings," she said pointing at her pink diamond studs then letting her hand fall to her lap.

"Come here," Amir said, scooting over to her and wrapping his arm around her shoulder. She leaned in, placing her head on his chest.

"I should've just given him the damn baby."

"Sacrificing the life you saw for yourself? Would that have made you happy?"

"I'd learn to be. At least I'd still be married."

"Yup, to a selfish motherfucker who clearly could care less about anyone else's joy besides his own."

"I'm studying to be a marriage therapist." Melodee let out an uneven sigh. "My parents have been married for 28-years, A.J. Do you know how humiliating it was having to tell them that Jaden and I were getting a divorce?"

"I can only imagine. I remember how much you adored their relationship. So much so, you refused to mess with anyone in high school because you felt they weren't marriage material."

Melodee pinched Amir on his arm and looked up at him. "Hush. It had nothing to do with them not being marriage material."

Amir laughed. "Well that's how you acted."

"Whatever," she said placing her head back on his chest. Her body pressed innocently against his fit like a puzzle piece as they sat in silence. Her mind was now preoccupied with thoughts of Jaden and his new woman. Who she was and where'd they met. Whether they'd met before he and Melodee started having problems. The thoughts became consuming. The vision of him with another woman made her feel a pulling sensation in the pit of her gut. Her emotions triggered a new batch of tears to form in her eyes.

Amir heard her sniffing back tears again and held her tighter, placing his chin on her head, then inhaling the sweet scent of her hair.

This wasn't the first time he'd held her close like this. Amir's arms soaked up many of her tears when they were in high school. Like when she got her heart broken by the guy she lost her virginity to and then again when she applied and didn't get into her first university choice, Spelman College, and thought she wouldn't be able to get into any other college.

"Aight, we need to lighten up the mood," Amir said in a low voice. "You still smoke?"

Amir had asked the magical question that would get her out of her blue state of mind.

Melodee perked right up, wiping the tears from her eyes as a smile pulled at her lips, then replied, "is water still wet?"

The flick of the lighter was like music to Melodee's ear when Amir lit the tip of the tightly rolled joint. Just like back in the day when they'd sneak out to smoke in her tree house, he'd skillfully cocooned weed in rolling paper, both of which he brought back with him from California, and that he kept in a locked safe in his bedroom. All it took was a knock on the terrace's sliding doors and a smoking gesture to Big Ant to get the weed out to them.

Just like back in the day, Amir sprinkled, licked and rolled the joint and Melodee watched on with folded legs and anticipation written all over her lips.

Two puffs and one pass was all it took for Melodee's thoughts of divorce to leave her mind and swirl overhead along with the cloud of marijuana smoke.

The two sat silently only communicating with their hand gestures, signaling the other to pass the rolled up weed between them. When she'd had enough, she used her foot to start the first of many cradle-like movements as the lounge chair swung with them on it. They both sat back with eyes fixed on the midnight sky as they moved back and forth.

"Still don't know how to roll, but love to smoke," Amir joked.

Melodee swatted him with her hand and he responded by poking her at her side.

It was like old times, just the two of them. Smoking in silence. No words needed. No explanations provided. Just being.

The munchies set in and stirred up their appetite, so Amir ordered up food that was nothing like the Doritos they used to eat after getting high. Mozzarella sticks, French fries, chicken fingers, and tiny tinfoils of strawberry shortcake lined the table in front of them. They scarfed down the food like it was their last supper.

With a mouth half full, Amir asked, "You ever wonder what happened to the stars?"

Melodee pointed her eyes up then back on him. "What do you mean?"

"In the sky." Amir pointed above them. "When we were kids, the stars used to be so bright now all I see is black sky."

Melodee looked up again at the blank sky then back at Amir and shrugged.

"What if the stars are extinct?"

Her eyebrows squished together. "Huh?"

"Like what if the sun is next?" he asked in a panic.

Melodee sucked her teeth then shoved him. "A.J., you're fucking up my high with this shit."

He laughed hysterically.

"You still do this? Talk about random stuff when you're high? Let's talk about something else, please."

Amir threw his hands up in the air mockingly conceding to her.

"I'm gonna be in a new movie."

Melodee looked at him with widened eyes and smiled big.

"That was what the business call earlier was all about. It's an action flick with an all-star cast, it's gonna be huge."

"That's so cool, A.J., I'm so happy for you! Doing what you always wanted to do," she said pulling him into a hug. "Just don't bomb in this one."

Amir pulled away. "What's that supposed to mean?"

Melodee tilted her head to the side and pursed her lips. "Two words: Red Room."

About two years back, Amir agreed to star in his first film, The Red Room, a horror flick where he acted as himself. The movie ended up flopping and Amir's acting was subpar.

"What about The Red Room?"

"The acting all around was bad. You weren't that bad but you weren't good either. You were playing yourself and you didn't do a good job at it."

Amir stared at her with his jaw slacked. "Did you just say that to my face?"

Melodee swallowed hard. "Sorry?"

"Everyone said I did good for my first time acting, but I felt I could have been better. Big Ant didn't even comment on it after seeing it so I already knew he hated it but didn't want to say it. You though," he said with a smile, "you just flat out said I was bad, damn."

"I'm sorry, A.J., I didn't mean it like that." Melodee's heart was beating fast with worry. "What I meant was—"

"No, it's cool. You were honest with me. I like that."

The smile that slowly spread across his lips made Melodee break eye contact, dropping her gaze down to the table of food.

"I can't have you thinking I'm a bad actor, though," he said, wiping his mouth then standing up. "Help me read my lines for this movie I'm about to do."

"For real?!"

"Yeah, you'll read the parts of my costar."

She clasped her hands over her chest, excited at the idea of reading a real life movie script. "Okay!"

For an hour, the two went back and forth reading lines from the script. Amir would say his lines and Melodee was responsible for saying the lines of Amir's female costar. The movie was about two assassins who'd been banned from their organizations for going against orders to assassinate the President of the United States. In the process of being on the run, they fall in love with each other when they least expect it.

They'd gotten to the middle of the script to a part where he and his costar are trapped in an abandoned warehouse. Melodee scanned ahead to keep track of the lines she had to say when she read in the summary that Amir and his costar would have to kiss in that scene.

Amir had just finished reading his line when he looked up at her waiting for her to read hers.

"It says we have to kiss right here." she pointed down at the script.

Amir chuckled. "Don't worry about that. We'll cross that bridge when we get there. Focus."

"Fine... but when we do get to that part, no tongue." She pointed at him.

They continued. Melodee found herself caught up in the scene. Amir did a great job at embodying the character. Changing up his mannerisms, adding the right amount of theatrics to his voice to make his character sound believable. By the time they got to the kissing scene, Melodee was all caught up.

Amir read his line. "I have to tell you something before it's too late."

"What is it," Melodee read.

"My feelings for you supersedes this mission. I've been fighting it for long enough but since there's no telling how much more time we have, I need to say this."

Melodee stared into his eyes lost in the emotion of the scene.

He cleared his throat then pointed his eyes down at the script then back at her, hinting for her to read her line.

"Oh, my bad," she said turning her eyes down on the script, "And what's that?"

"I'm in love with you."

They were only words, scripted words, but there was something about the way he said those words that made her skip a breath. With the script, still in hand, he leaned in her direction. Amir used the tip of his finger to move a few of her loose curls out of the way as he pressed his lips against hers. Instinctively, she closed her eyes. It was just a peck, no tongue just as she asked, but it still sent her body surging with pleasure. Him simply pressing his soft warm lips against hers made her shiver and caused goosebumps to sleeve her bare legs and arms.

He sat back in his seat on the lounge chair and the two looked at each other. Melodee was breathing heavier and Amir could tell this by the rise and fall of her breasts in her plunging V-neck romper. His eyes darted from left to right trying to read her like the script he held in his hand.

She couldn't believe the heat radiating between her thighs for him. Her longing for another touch. But it couldn't be by just anyone, she needed to be touched by him.

He read her mind.

The script he was holding dropped to the terrace's cement floor in front of them when he slid closer to her. He pressed his hands to her cheek. She closed her eyes. Then he brushed his lips against hers. He'd only glide his tongue past her lips and into her mouth when she parted her lips to meet his tongue with hers. Their tongues met, twirled, then stroked one another. Amir moved one hand off her cheek and slid it down her lower back, pressing his palm at the base of her spine to push her closer to him. He moaned on her lips, surprised she let him get this close to her. He wanted more.

Their tongues swirled over the other, muffled moans and puckering sounds of them kissing were drowned out by the rush of traffic below them. He reached down to pull her legs free from their folded position. She was open now for him to lean her back and take her deeper into their kiss. The minute he lowered his bodyweight on top of her, this jolted her right out of the moment.

She pressed her hands into the cushion of the lounge chair to balance herself to sit back up, pulling her legs closer to herself and bringing her fingers to her lips. Her heavy breaths were audible and so was his. She glanced down at his lap only for a second to see his slacks failing to hold back his erection.

Melodee was hot and she was beyond ready. But bigger than that, she was confused.

With brows pulled in together she asked, "were you still acting?"

Amir glided the side of his finger under his wet lip and said nothing.

"Because that felt real," she added.

"What do you think?" he asked.

For the first time Melodee experienced what other women felt when they looked at Amir, horniness. She was seeing bedroom eyes, a hard dick, and an opportunity to get the release her body's been missing as a recently divorced woman. These were feelings that were new to her when she thought of their friendship.

"I think you're trying to get an Academy Award," she answered.

Everything about him was a sight to see. From the way his shirt laid flat against his chest to the veins in his hands and forearms visible courtesy of his rolled up sleeves. The way he looked at her and his smile was sending her body temperature to a fever high.

Noticing where her gaze was, on the stiffness between his legs, he took his chance.

"You want to take this to my bedroom?"

A bemused smile pulled at her lips and she leaned forward to playfully nudge Amir on the shoulder with her hand. "Wow. So, that's how you get the ladies to come up out their panties."

Amir burst out laughing.

"You wanna take this to my room?" she mocked trying to imitate his voice. "That was a good play, A.J. If I didn't know you well enough—"

"But I'm not playing with you, Mel."

He licked his lips before bringing his bottom lip into his mouth and briefly holding it in place with his top teeth.

"Mmm," she moaned to herself. For a moment, she considered the prospect of letting him have her in that way. She quickly shooed the idea from her mind, shaking her head. "I gotta go."

Amir frowned. "Right now?"

Melodee had one foot already in her strappy heels as she tried her best to steady her trembling hands to clasp the buckle shut.

"Oh yes... right now."

"Then I'll take you home."

"No! You need to stay here."

He laughed, his eyes back to admiring the shape of his friend's legs and the curve in her thigh.

When she noticed his silence, she glanced over her shoulder to catch him visually stripping her naked, again. She balled her hand into a fist then tried to punch him on the leg but he moved out of the way.

"I told you to stop looking at me like that, A.J."

"I can't help it, Mel, damn. If you see what I see you'd be staring, too."

She strapped on her other sandal and stood to her feet.

This is not happening, she thought to herself.

She tried to rush toward the terrace's sliding doors but he blocked her exit.

"At least let me have my driver take you home. I'm not liking the idea of you getting in a cab this late."

"I'm a big girl, A.J."

He grabbed her hand and she tried to pull her hand loose, but he held on refusing to let her go.

Amir turned her to face him then tilted her chin so she could look up at him. Her knees knocked.

"Please let my driver take you home, I'm begging you."

She thought about it for a moment and figured it didn't matter who took her home if it wasn't him. So, she agreed.

As Amir's chauffeured Maybach Landaulet whizzed down the expressway with instructions to drop her to DUMBO Brooklyn where her condo was, she eased her head out the window that was lowered down all the way. Bitter cold air chilled her face and slightly chapped her lips but she didn't care, she needed the cold relief.

When they pulled off from the curb in front of Amir's loft, she asked the driver to lower the back windows, all of them. He of course thought it was an odd request given the freezing temperature outside but Melodee needed a cold blast of air to cool down after what took place between she and Amir.

Her body was hot with desire, replaying their kiss like one of those online gifs. The touch of his hands against her cheeks. His scent. The way he looked her in the eyes and spoke to her in fluent body language.

Melodee ran her finger along the seam of her lips. She'd just kissed the one man women all over the world would give their left nipple to kiss knowing there was a possibility he'd touch the right.

She blushed at the thought.

Her hand came to her neck as the cool breeze finally lowered the heat emanating from her body. That was when the tip of her finger grazed her right ear. It was a subtle touch, but it was enough for her to notice one of her earrings were missing.

She almost swallowed her tongue as she pinched her left earlobe and then her right. That was the one that was bare. Melodee looked below her feet. There was nothing but soft white carpeting. She unhooked her seatbelt and turned in her seat, running her hand over the buttery leather, forcing her fingers into the back of the cushion. She knew there was no way the earring could have fallen so deep in the chair so soon.

Melodee wrung her hands. Her mind mentally retraced her steps that night, her face set with furrowed brows. She immediately removed the other diamond stud and dropped it in her bag. She cursed at herself for deciding to wear the earrings that night. As her insurance plan, the earrings were worth very little if they weren't sold together. With plans to quit her receptionist job, she'd have to work overtime to save up the money the diamonds were worth to be able to leave and not be strapped for cash.

Where the hell did I lose my earring? she wondered.

But it was obvious. So obvious, it went right over her head.

Chapter Six

The next day just before noon, Melodee sat across from Sheena trying her best to keep up with their conversation. They were at brunch at a quaint hole-in-the-wall seafood shack across the street from Brooklyn's Coney Island amusement park. The seafood shack was styled in red, white, and blue decor with wooden tables and chairs inside the restaurant and picnic-style tables outside. Inside and out of the restaurant smelled like an authentic seafood house. Seasoned lobster tails, shrimp, and scallops sizzled on the grill while patrons waited in line to either pickup or place their orders. The hum of chatter and laughter floated around Melodee and Sheena like the white clouds overhead as they sat outside at a table with an iconic view of Coney Island's Cyclone rollercoaster and Deno's Wonder Wheel.

It was an unseasonably warm December day. The temperature around fifty degrees. But even if the snow piled up in front of them, eating outside would be Melodee and Sheena's first choice. They loved the view too much to let the winter air force them inside.

Melodee sipped on her mimosa as Sheena blabbed about a documentary she and her husband Ray watched when she returned home from Club Déjà Vu the night before. Melodee managed a few *uh-huh's* and convincing head nods that made Sheena believe she was having a two-way conversation. Melodee's physical body might have been sitting across from her best friend but her mind was still on that terrace lounge chair with Amir at his loft.

His soft lips on hers was such a vivid memory, she ran the tip of her finger along the fullest part of her lips where he'd kissed her. It was hot to the touch. She swallowed her mimosa whole and gestured politely to the waitress to bring another carafe of champagne and orange juice to their table.

"You're thirsty, huh?" Sheena asked as she stuffed another succulent crab cake into her mouth, her fifth one since they arrived at brunch.

"And you're hungry. Can you leave me some, please?" Melodee joked.

Sheena giggled. "So how was Amir's after, after-party last night? You promised to tell me what happened, but you didn't even call me when you got back home."

Melodee cleared her throat reaching for her glass of water and chugged only stopping when the glass was empty.

"I got back late and didn't want to wake you. The party was nice, though."

"What's his place look like?" Sheena asked. She was turned in her seat facing Melodee giving Melodee her full attention.

"Big," Melodee replied.

"Were there celebrities at his loft?"

"I saw familiar faces."

Sheena's brows arched as she waited for Melodee to continue with more details. But she didn't.

"When I asked you to tell me everything, I didn't mean like this. Telling me his loft was big, and you saw familiar faces tells me nothing."

"There was nothing special about the place and nothing really happened once I got to the loft," Melodee lied. In that moment, she had a mental flashback of her and Amir's first kiss. How for the first time she'd seen sex in his eyes when he looked at her. It was hard for her to deny to herself that seeing him in that way turned her on immensely. Unbeknown to her, while she was busy recollecting, her lips were slowly curving into a smile while her eyes sparkled, catching a glint of light from the sun.

Sheena saw it all and smiled with Melodee. "You're smiling. What's that about?"

Melodee straightened her posture in her seat, then reached for the black pepper grinder, sprinkling the spice onto her lobster roll. "I'm not smiling?"

Sheena's lips turned down into a frown.

"I knew it. I knew this would happen between the two of you when you agreed to go to that party." Sheena glared at Melodee with tight lips.

The breath of air Melodee inhaled stirred in the back of her throat as she held her breath. She stroked her eyebrow with the pad of her finger, visibly worried. Her stomach fluttered like a net of butterflies had been released into her abdomen.

Melodee lowered her gaze onto her lap. "Sheena, I'm sorry. I didn't—"

"I knew you would be friends with him again, ugh! Y'all were so close back in the day and now he's all rich and famous so of course you'd want to be cool again. I knew this would happen."

Sheena picked up her napkin and patted her lips before tossing the napkin down on the table and folding her arms in front of her.

Melodee let out a long exhale and flopped back in her seat, relieved. A shaky laugh left her mouth as she poured herself another glass of mimosa.

"So y'all best friends again, huh? Because you know I'd hate that, right? Especially after the shit he put me through."

"Um..."

"It's because of him I can't carry a child... you know that, right? That abortion he forced me to have made my cervix weak. The doctor said so."

Melodee pinched the skin on her throat and leaned back in her chair.

"It makes me so sick just knowing that if I didn't get rid of the baby or even gotten pregnant by Amir, I could've had my baby already with Ray."

"Uh..." Melodee struggled to find the words to say.

"That fucking asshole. I hate him."

With that, Sheena reached for one of the last crab cakes and ate it whole. She chewed the fishcake hard looking away from Melodee and into the distance toward the Wonder Wheel. Her jaw was so tense, arms folded tight, if they were in a cartoon, steam would blow from Sheena's ears, too.

Any chance Melodee had of telling Sheena about she and Amir went up in smoke with Sheena's fiery response.

Melodee reached for the remaining crab cake and stuffed it in her mouth, deciding right then that what happened between she and Amir was nothing and had to stay between them two.

It was just a kiss, anyway, Melodee rationalized to herself while swallowing her mimosa in two gulps.

Chapter Seven

Throats clearing and the turning of textbook pages kept Melodee from falling asleep as she sat in a small nook in her university's library. Day had not yet broken but the sky began turning a soft color of blue with peach-colored clouds.

It was a Friday, one week after New Year's Eve and two weeks after she and Amir kissed. She'd spent her New Year's Eve in bed, purposely falling asleep before the clock struck twelve. A little part of her expected Jaden to call her to wish her a Happy New Year but the only people she heard from were her parents and Sheena.

Earlier that morning, she bought a large cup of coffee from the student coffee shop, which she tilted in front of her lips to sip slow to help stay awake. She needed something to aid her in her early morning studies before heading out to work.

At around 7 a.m., she glanced down at the time on her phone and sighed. She gathered her books and slid them into her brown leather satchel and made her way to the exit.

For the next eight-hours, Melodee will be like a slave to her boss Dr. Sherida Pierce. Sherida was a marriage therapist with an office in a small ten floor building on Park Avenue South in Manhattan. Everything was tiny about her private office including Sherida herself. But what she lacked in size she made up for in attitude. And this was exactly the reason Melodee hated going to work.

After Jaden moved out of their condo leaving little doubt that they would move forward with their divorce, Melodee was forced into getting a job while going to school full-time at New York University. She had to balance work with school, needing to excel at both. It was difficult for her, her first month since she was a year away from receiving her PhD and had research and teaching obligations to meet. But she got used to it and learned how to manage by reorganizing her schedule and drinking a lot of coffee.

She interviewed with Sherida for a receptionist position and had to come back for two more interviews before Sherida agreed to hire her.

Two hours after arriving to the office, Melodee reached into her brown satchel to pull out her psychology textbook like she always did. With no clients in the office and no appointments scheduled for that day, she kept herself busy by studying during the times the phone didn't ring.

Melodee's desk was located just outside of Sherida's office door, a door Sherida insisted stay open whenever the office was empty.

In her office, Sherida's degrees and awards lined the shelves behind her desk. She kept succulent plants on her desk and once insisted Melodee do the same. But when the plants on Melodee's desk kept dying in Melodee's care, Sherida stopped suggesting it.

Melodee had to keep her desk plain with just a laptop to schedule appointments, a phone to take calls, and one note pad and a pen to jot down any random things Sherida needed Melodee to pass along to her assistant.

A few minutes after Melodee highlighted paragraphs in her textbook, the office phone rang.

"Hey, Mel, it's me," Amir said on the other end of the phone.

"A.J.?" Melodee replied, turning to look over her shoulder toward Sherida's office. "How'd you get this number?"

He chuckled. "I remember you mentioning your boss's name that night on the terrace, so I had my assistant look up her office number."

"Oh. Well, I can't talk," she whispered.

"Melodee?" Sherida called from her office.

Melodee exhaled loudly into the phone then said, "I have to go."

"Why?"

"Because I can't take personal calls on this line. My boss hates that."

"Just tell her you're talking to me. I'm sure she won't mind."

She couldn't see his face, but judging by the tone in his voice she could tell he was grinning slyly when he said that.

She smiled. "You could be President Barack Obama calling and she would still care less. She's not down for personal calls, period."

"Is that a personal call, Melodee?" Sherida asked from her office.

The sound of Sherida's chair sliding against her patterned carpeted office floor gave hint she stood up from her desk.

"I gotta go," Melodee said with her finger moving over the button to end the call.

"One second. I'm on a two-day break from the tour and I'm in New York. Can you come to my loft, tonight?"

"I can't," Melodee said glancing over her shoulder again.

"Why not?"

"I just can't, A.J. I'm gonna hang up, now."

Truthfully, Melodee was nervous about being alone with Amir again. After her talk with Sheena and Sheena's refusal to bite her tongue about Amir, Melodee decided she'd need to keep her distance from him to keep the peace with her girl. Especially if she and Amir's relationship was becoming something more than just a platonic friendship.

"Melodee, is that a client?" Sherida asked, her voice inching closer to her office door.

"Later, A.J."

"I got your earring. That pink diamond stud you were wearing the other night. You dropped it on the terrace... probably when we were about to get busy." He laughed.

Melodee pulled the chord of the phone and ducked her head underneath her desk. She gave a sigh of relief. "Thank God! It's at your loft?"

"Yup. So… you're gonna come and get it, right?"

Those earrings were everything at that time especially since Melodee had plans to quit her job to focus entirely on school. Working at the doctor's office and going to school full-time was a stress. She wasn't sleeping as much and it had been affecting her grades. With only one more year before graduation she had to do what was necessary to stay on track to graduate. Plus, Sherida had begun working the last nerve Melodee had left so she wasn't sure how much longer she'd be able to continue working for her before snapping.

"Melodee!" Sherida sneered. She was standing in front of Melodee's desk and directly over her now. Her deep-set eyes shaped like large brown almonds were like daggers staring down at Melodee. She folded her arms over her white dress shirt that was buttoned all the way to her neck as she tapped her brown square toe heels on the hardwood floor beneath them.

"Fine. I'll be there tonight," Melodee said into the phone before placing the phone down on its base.

"I thought you understood when I told you no personal calls."

"I know, Sherida. I'm so sorry, but—"

"That's Dr. Pierce to you," Sherida corrected.

Melodee sighed heavily then pressed her lips together, pulling air through her nose to calm herself. "My apologies, Dr. Pierce. It was a quick call and—"

"I don't care if it was a millisecond long. When I say no personal calls, I mean no personal calls. My clients could have been calling at the same time you were yapping on my phone about God knows what. They could have been in distress."

"It won't happen again," Melodee assured.

"It better not," Sherida glared with wide eyes before walking away and returning to her office.

Melodee plopped down on to her desk chair and brought her hands to her forehead. She would definitely go to Amir's loft to get that earring because if she really wanted to pawn the studs, they'd only be worth something as a pair.

Chapter Eight

The moment Melodee stepped off the elevator, she could hear music playing behind the closed doors of Amir's loft. It was a song she'd never heard before, but it sounded amazing. Sung over live instruments, Amir's vocals sounded crisp and unique. She knocked on the door and within seconds he opened it. He was shirtless, wearing just a pair of black sweatpants. Her eyes glided over the lean strong muscles of his arms and the defined lines on his abdomen. By the time their eyes met, he was grinning at her, his body leaning against the door and blocking her entrance.

"Go put on a shirt," she told him.

Her body was doing that thing again, tingling. Although it was below thirty degrees outside, he was making her sweat by just looking at him.

"Hello to you, too," he said stepping to the side so she could walk through the door. She didn't move.

"I'm not playing with you. Go put a shirt on, A.J."

His grin turned into a smile and she shut her eyes tight and sighed.

"You think the effect I'm having on you right now will be different if I put on a shirt?"

"I'm not coming in there unless you put on a shirt."

She knew her reaction was a little ridiculous, but she also couldn't believe how her body had a mind of its own in his presence. Melodee couldn't control the ache between her thighs that was demanding all her attention and damn near screaming at her to give Amir permission to touch her there and everywhere else.

"Fine." He left the door and walked farther into the loft. "I'll get a shirt. Come in and shut the door."

So, she did. The loft looked bigger than it did the night she attended his party. The ceilings were higher and the decor more vibrant. His tastes were all over the loft's decor. From the paintings of instruments and classic singers like Billie Holiday and Etta James to his immaculate entertainment center complete with the bigger than life flat screen she saw the other night.

Next to his built-in fireplace was his acoustic guitar. The same guitar he'd walk down the school halls with strapped to his back. She recognized it because his initials, A.J., were in the same spot. He carved them into the body of the guitar with his house keys in her tree house during one of their smoking sessions.

He returned wearing a white shirt as requested. Amir splayed his arms as he walked down his glass staircase, stopping on the bottom step and turning in Melodee's direction.

"Is this better?"

"Yes, thank you."

He laughed.

She sat down on his long cream-colored couch, leaning forward to unlace her black and white Converses. She was removing them not to get comfortable, but out of respect for his home and not bringing in the dirt from the sidewalk outside.

Her head nodded in time to the beat of the song that was playing. The chorus was catchy, and she'd already memorized the words and was humming along with it.

"Is this new?"

"What?" he asked from the kitchen. He was pouring white zinfandel into two wine glasses.

"This song."

He walked the glasses over to where Melodee was sitting, placing them down on the hand-blown glass coffee table in front of her then sat next to her.

"Yeah."

She gasped. "Off your new album?!"

He nodded.

Melodee pressed her hand against her chest and smiled big. According to the conversation the two gentlemen had in Amir's kitchen the night of Amir's party, no one had heard the album other than the executives at Dope Records.

"I heard you weren't allowing anyone to listen to this other than your label executives."

"You're not just anyone."

The two sipped their wine as they continued listening to two more of Amir's album cuts. He was explaining the inspiration behind the songs, where he wrote them, and why he chose them for the album. Listening to him speak as a creative was inspiring to Melodee. She sat with clasped hands to her chest, eyes wide and bright as she hung on to his every word.

"I got one song I want to add to Black Rose before we release it," he added as they finished the last of their wine.

"A song you wrote?"

He shook his head, picking up the glasses and taking it back to the kitchen. His kitchen was huge. He had a stainless steel Sub-Zero fridge which was the size of a refrigerator you'd find in a gourmet restaurant. The counter top was made of black granite and gleamed beneath the kitchen's swinging overhead light.

"No, a cover," he answered.

"Of what?"

"Al Green's 'Simply Beautiful.' I figured since the critics are always comparing me and saying I sound like a new school Al Green, I'd give them a little something to talk about."

Melodee reached for her bag in search of her phone. "I don't think I've heard that one before. Maybe I have but don't remember how it goes. I'll search for it online."

"I'll do you one better," he said walking over to his fireplace and picking up his guitar.

With it in hand, he walked around the coffee table and sat opposite Melodee.

She couldn't help the smile stretching her lips as she watched him tune his instrument, strumming the strings and turning the tuning pegs on the headstock. Once it was ready, he strummed the opening melody of "Simply Beautiful."

His voice was like a warm hug. Soothing, masculine, and endearing.

She folded her legs Indian style, propped her elbow on her thigh and leaned her cheek in her opened hand as she attentively watched and listened to him sing.

When his eyes weren't closed, absorbed in the song, or looking down at his guitar whenever he needed to change chords, he kept his gaze on her as he sang each word. She maintained firm eye contact herself stroking her arm as she swayed from side to side to his playing.

The minute the song ended all Melodee could do was clap.

"Your singing has gotten so damn good over the years. That was amazing."

"I know." He chuckled cockily. Amir leaned back to place the guitar on its back behind the coffee table.

He stood up, rubbed his palms together, and asked, "wanna smoke?"

Melodee bit her lip in thought. She remembered what happened the last time they shared a joint alone. But Melodee never liked passing up stellar weed which she knew Amir had in his stash.

"The answer will always be yes." She smiled.

It was an hour later and the two were as high as the needle on top of the Empire State Building. Melodee laid flat on her back her head on the armrest of the couch, her legs and socked-feet extended on Amir's lap. His head lolled over the back of his sofa as their talk drifted to memories of high school. In their trip down memory lane, they recalled the times as sophomores when their English teacher Mr. Grimes was absent on Fridays and they'd have a lazy substitute.

This substitute teacher, Ms. Donaldson, couldn't care less about their education and would sometimes leave them alone to step out of the school's building to smoke a cigarette during school hours. In her absence, the classroom of hormonal teens would keep themselves busy by playing several rounds of truth or dare.

"And you'd never pick dare, always truth," Amir recollected.

Melodee smiled to herself remembering those times. It was around this time she introduced Amir to Sheena.

"Ya damn right!" she replied. "I would not choose dare and have you boys stick your tongues in my mouth after kissing three girls before me."

He laughed. "Not true. It wasn't about getting dared to kiss all the time." He was quiet for a moment before saying, "I always wanted you to choose dare with me."

Melodee cleared her throat and sat up removing her legs off Amir. He glanced over at her noticing her discomfort and sighed.

"What is it now?"

"Nothing," she lied. She ran the palms of her hands over her fitted jeans, a nervous habit.

"You always did that."

"Did what?"

"Get uncomfortable when I put you and me in a sentence."

Melodee shook her head.

"Yeah, it's true. I told you I was falling for you our sophomore year that night in your tree house, you reacted by introducing me to Sheena the next day. Telling me she likes me."

"You seemed like you wanted a girlfriend so I figured she'd be a better fit. Plus, she really liked you, A.J."

Amir shook his head. "So, you ignore that I said in bold words that I was feeling you." He pointed at her. "And how you gon' decide who's a good fit for me, anyway?"

"A.J.—"

"Don't A.J. me," he said poking her on her side.

She rolled her eyes and turned to face him. "Okay, let's say I chose dare when we played in Mr. Grimes' class. What would you have dared me to do?"

"I don't know. Let's try it right now."

He smiled at her and her heart skipped a beat. She glanced at the time on his gold-plated wall clock. It was close to midnight. She'd spent more than enough time at his place.

"Fine. I'll play your little game. After that I have to go."

"Truth or dare."

She raised her hand in surrender and replied, "dare."

He smiled that big sexy smile that secretly drove her insane.

"I dare you to kiss me, again."

Melodee kissed her teeth. "Then you want to tell me the dares weren't always about getting kissed."

"It wasn't. But I'm daring you to do it. So do it."

Their eyes met as she shifted uncomfortably in her seat, again. She could hear her heart beating so hard it mimicked the drums in Amir's song playing in the background.

He licked his lips and gave her those same inviting, come-and-get-it eyes he did on the terrace the night of his party.

Her body was hypersensitive, a shiver sending her into a brief shake.

She asked, "What are you trying to do?"

He released a sigh. "So, what? You came over here only for your earring? The earring your ex-husband gave you?"

"It's bigger than him giving it to me. I need them."

"For what?"

"All you need to know is that I need them, okay? Damn."

"You're not a jewelry person. They're your favorite color, but I know that's not why you want it back. You're not even wearing any jewelry right now. So, I know it's not because you're in love with them."

"You remembered that?" she asked.

"What?"

"That my favorite color is pink."

"Of course."

Melodee got quiet.

"Is it the money?" Amir continued probing. "I can give you the money, Mel, you know that. I got plenty of it. No amount is too big for me. You need it, I got you. Forget those earrings. They're trash. I can buy you bigger diamonds than that."

She shook her head and jumped to her feet, frustrated at what he was implying.

"I don't want your money, A.J.," she spat.

He clenched his jaw and stood up too. "Fine. You want the damn earring? It's in my room... up there." He pointed.

Amir turned on his bare soles and walked toward his glass staircase that led up to one of his bedrooms. He looked over his shoulder to see Melodee still standing by the couch. "If you want the earring you have to come with me to get it."

Melodee took a deep breath and blew the air out of her mouth.

"Come on, Mel," he said walking up the stairs.

She found him in his bedroom with his nightstand drawer open. She watched as he reached down into it, spotting a box of magnums inside as well. It was opened, its foil contents spilling out into the drawer. On the other nightstand near where Melodee stood, were two partially melted white candles. Between them was a glass framed photo of Amir's late mother, Anita.

He walked back over to where Melodee was standing, with her earring in his palm, and held it out for her to take. She reached for it and he closed his hand and pulled it away.

"Aight, look. You can take this earring and be stuck in your past or you can forget about it and choose me instead and make me your future."

Her brows wrinkled. "A.J., stop playing."

"I want you, Mel."

She shook her head, "No. I could never do that to—"

"To who? Sheena?"

Melodee looked away.

"That was twelve years ago, Melodee. You realize that, right? We're about to be thirty in three years. You're telling me a relationship that happened in high school is stopping this between you and me? Me and Sheena are so far in the past."

"You don't understand."

"Make me understand... please!" he begged.

She couldn't tell him if she wanted to, anyway. Sheena had already made Melodee promise not to tell Amir anything about her pregnancy complications when they met up that day in Coney Island. He knew of the abortion but he didn't know the problems it created for Sheena who's been having trouble conceiving. Sheena would be angry if Melodee told Amir something so personal.

"I can't."

He walked up to her, and she stepped back. She kept stepping back until she couldn't anymore because of the wall that was now behind her. With her back against the wall, he got close, placing the earring in his sweatpants pocket and planting both of his palms against the wall on opposite sides of Melodee's body. Amir's gaze dropped to her chest that was rising and falling with each breath she took. He looked her right in her eyes, trying to read her again.

"I can't give you what you want, A.J.," she whispered.

"Yes, you can. You're the only one I want it from."

He backed away and took her hand, leading her over to his bed. When they got close, she pulled her hand free.

Amir sighed before dropping himself down on the bed and moving to the edge. He sat with his legs wide, propping his elbows on top of his knees. He dropped his head into his hands and said, "I just wanna love you. Why don't you let me do that?"

"You're my best friend's ex-boyfriend. You got her pregnant for God's sake. Y'all got too much history for us to ever have anything together."

"That's bullshit."

"That's a fact," she retorted.

"I was your friend before I had anything to do with Sheena. That should count for something, no?"

He leaned forward and grabbed her hand, pulling her to him. She resisted by trying to pull her hand free again but he was determined and held on to her.

Melodee stood between his legs and over him as he ran his hands down the side of her jeans and over her hips.

He took her left hand into his and fiddled with her ring finger that still bared the tan line from her wedding band.

She closed her eyes tight, shifting her weight from one leg to the other when the throbbing between her thighs became too distracting. Her body begged for her to give in to him while her conscience put up a good fight.

"I like the way things are with us and intimacy has a way with ruining things between people who care about each other. This would change everything, A.J. Our friendship wouldn't be the same anymore."

"Good. I don't want it to be the same. I'm not looking to be your friend anymore, Mel. I was your friend in high school and that was enough back then. We're grown now. A higher power brought you back in my life at the right time, can't you see that?" He glanced at the photo of his mother sitting on his nightstand. "So now, I want to be your man. I've always wanted to be that to you and you know that."

He interlocked his fingers with hers. "Your ex-husband," he said with so much intensity in his voice it resonated in her soul, "he did shit like make you cry. I can see you're still hurting from your divorce and that kills me to know this. You see me, I'll never abandon you. I promise to never do that to you. What I will do is make you smile until your face hurts. I'll smudge your lipstick because I won't be able to resist the urge to kiss you." He grinned when he looked up at her. "And I'll definitely mess up your hair a lot while we make love. I apologize for that in advance."

Melodee giggled under her breath.

His hands were back on her hips which he used to pull her closer to him. He leaned forward and pressed his lips against the v-shaped crease that separated her thighs in her jeans, kissing her there.

She gasped.

He looked up into her eyes. "I want to make you do more of that, right there."

Amir slowly moved his hand up her t-shirt, running his palm over her bare abdomen. She bit her bottom lip as she watched with bated breath as he continued to seduce her.

"I want to make you moan... real loud," he said before grinning at her. "I want to see what you look like coming, every time I mend my body with yours," he told her. "So, you're right. Us doing this will change everything. But that's what I want, and that's what we need."

His hands grasped the outer curve of her thigh to pull her closer and into the position to straddle him.

"Please," he pleaded with her, leaning back on the bed so that he could lower her down on top of him.

She broke eye contact and placed her hand against his shoulder to push herself away.

"Look at me, Mel," he told her.

She closed her eyes and sighed in defeat before opening them again. Their eyes met and the look he gave her was irresistible. She started breathing harder, her hands shaking, her body craving his next touch. In that moment, she knew she couldn't ignore the feelings she had for him that she'd kept under control.

"Stop fighting this and give in to me," he said.

They held their stares for what felt like forever. The longer she looked into his light brown eyes, the more aroused she became. So, she conceded.

"Okay," she whispered, right before straddling him.

Amir having waited so long for that moment wasted no time. A shaky sigh expelled from her lips as he steadied his hands to smooth up her t-shirt and over her bra, cupping and massaging her breasts.

She let her head fall back as his hands continued its erotic exploration up and down her torso.

Then she submitted completely. She allowed herself to give in, just as he asked by surrendering to his touch. She moaned as the pads of his fingers glided over her, kneading and caressing her soft skin. He paid attention to her reactions, watching her attentively and notating mentally what made her moan the loudest as if he'd be quizzed on it later.

Amir peeled her clothes off nice and slow, taking visual snapshots of her curves for later thoughts of her. Once she was nude, he slipped out of his clothes and laid beside her. The heat was on but even if it weren't they'd still stay warm from them touching each other.

The two looked each other over, optically digesting their nude figures, as they saw each other in the flesh for the first time.

"God, you're beautiful," he told her.

He couldn't take the wait any longer and brushed his lips against hers, kissing her with every ounce of passion he could muster up to give. His hands stayed busy between her legs massaging inside her lower lips and around her erogenous zones using her juices as lubricant, rubbing her close to her first orgasm.

Like he wanted she moaned, louder, and it was the sweetest sound to him.

Soon their bodies were joined like puzzle pieces but in a different way. She gasped at the point of penetration and he kissed her, twirling his tongue around hers. The moment she opened around his sheathed erection, the wetness between her thighs eased his passage.

Their relationship transformed like a hologram as he moved back and forth, in then out between her thighs. He watched her as she bit her lips beneath him. How she gasped for air that was already there when he moved deeper into her. The way her face was set in her sexiest expression. It turned him on knowing she was enjoying him. Her inner walls gripped around him like a tailored glove and a whisper of a groan escaped his lips.

Their picture-perfect friendship was in the same frame, but their relationship was a different image now.

He moved slow, his pace building like the rising crescendo of one of his songs. The simple act of him gliding between her wet walls made her cling to him. Their eyes stayed on each other, watching as their pupils dilated until the sight of seeing their faces contort in response to the way the other was serving pleasure made them too weak to maintain their stares.

They bit their lips in lust, licked and hid them as the sheets wrinkled beneath them.

Amir's album played on repeat in the background and he delivered his strokes to the rhythm of the bass. Making love to one of his songs had always been a fantasy of his and the fact that he did it with someone he cared so much for made the moment even more significant.

Melodee's moans filled the space the music missed, echoing throughout the loft.

Amir was a silent lover, letting his satisfaction be known through the heavy breaths that left his body and the way his eyes rolled to the back of his head when he climaxed.

When he still wanted more, he turned her over and laid behind her. He pushed past her slick opening with the thrust of his hips, hands-free. She met each of his methodical movements by pressing back on him. She was in heaven, her body on fire, clenching and releasing as he sexed her from the back. Amir showered her neck and shoulders with kisses while his fingers played a disappearing act between her lower lips. He stroked her clit with his finger as he glided in and out of her, skilled enough to do both simultaneously without falling out of sync.

The way he moved sent her pulse racing, body shaking, the volume of her moans elevated.

"Oh, God…yes," she moaned as Amir served her sublime injections from behind.

Soon his lips journeyed down her back flipping her over when he wanted a taste. The warm tip of his tongue found its way between her thighs where he French kissed her clit. Her heart raced and her muscles trembled. After she shuddered on his lips, he laid flat on his back.

"Show me what you got, baby," he said, lifting her up into the position to straddle him. "Ride me."

Amir's fingers roamed every curve of her body and were like magic as she moved over him. His touch sent her to an almost out-of-body experience as she circled her hips on top.

He left her speechless, and she left him breathless. Her body vibrating on top of his and his fingertips digging into her hips to hold her steady so he could continue to penetrate her as she came with him still inside of her.

Like the girls at his party mentioned, he held up all night. But Melodee never tired, always ready for the next position he pulled her into.

She got more than enough and felt almost greedy when her eyes slid open before day broke and she reached for him for an encore performance. Her fingers crawled beneath the covers in search of his dick, griping him with her palm and fingers then whispering for more in his ear.

He gave her more. A lot more. So much more her voice was hoarse by morning from moaning so loud.

Finally sated they fell asleep. Their bodies coiled as one. With her back against his chest, Melodee laid nestled in Amir's arms, her head on his bicep, his left knee between her thighs. He held her so close he made it impossible to tell their dewy brown skins apart.

Melodee awoke to the clinking and clanking of chinaware downstairs in Amir's kitchen. The sunlight from outside glowed bright behind the custom-made drapes in his bedroom. She sat up quick and glanced at the clock on his bedroom wall. It was 9:15am. She sighed, relieved that she still had three hours before meeting up with Sheena for her doctor's appointment.

That thought caused a frown to weigh down her lips. She would have to see her friend after sleeping with the man who was the reason she needed to see her OBGYN every month. Melodee reached behind her to find only the folds of the white sheets. She inhaled the aroma of eggs and something sweet like pancakes wafting from the kitchen downstairs. A gratifying moan left her lips as she rolled off the bed, grabbing Amir's white tee he wore the night before and pulling it on to cover herself. In his bathroom, she found a folded towel and one of those generic packaged toothbrushes you find in hotel bathrooms. She wrinkled her eyebrows at how neatly placed her morning essentials appeared. It was clear to her that Amir had done this morning-after routine many times before.

After freshening up, she walked down the glass staircase to find Amir, shirtless with only a pair of black silk pajama pants on. He stood in his large kitchen and over a massive breakfast spread as he watched her walk down the stairs. On his black granite kitchen island were plates of omelets, one made with vegetables the other meat.

There were bagels, crepes, fresh fruits, shrimp with grits, and three carafes filled to the brim with three different juices.

"Damn," was all Melodee said as she got to the bottom of the staircase and stared at the spread impressed. "You made all of this for me?"

He told her, "I wish I could take all the credit. I had my chef hook this up for you, though. I wasn't sure what you liked or hated so I made him cook all this. Don't worry about finishing everything. Whatever we don't touch I'll have my assistant pick up and take to the shelters."

Melodee sat at the stool on the opposite side of the island and plucked one grape from its bunch tossing it into her mouth. "This looks like he took a long time to prepare all of this."

"He's on-call so he was here early."

They looked at each other for the first time after making love the night before. Amir licked his lips and Melodee looked away shyly.

"So..." he said to her.

Her eyes fell on his toned abs and his medium build arms and she sighed. Memories of the night before made her clasp her thighs together. "Are we going to have an awkward morning-after?"

He rounded the island, walking over to where she sat and took a seat on the stool beside her. "Nah. Last night was..."Amit blew air from his mouth. He bit his bottom lip with attraction as he looked down at her bare thighs.

"Amazing." She finished his sentence. "At least for me."

"For me, too." He leaned over to kiss her on her neck and she giggled.

On her neck, he whispered, "Can we do it again?"

"Um," she said looking away and directing her attention to the plate with the vegetable omelet, placing it down in front of herself, "I have to meet up with Sheena in a few hours."

"Oh," he said leaning away. Amir scratched the center of his curly top fade and Melodee looked on while forking a chunk of the omelet into her mouth. "I want to talk to you about the abortion."

Melodee's food almost slipped down the wrong pipe when she tried to object in haste. With a full mouth, she said, "A.J., you don't have to do that."

"Yes, I do. I'm serious when I say I want something with you, Mel. I don't want last night to be a one night thing. It's so much bigger than that. What I gave to you last night, there's a lot more where that came from." He smirked before his frown weighed on his lips.

Melodee stayed silent. She reached for the carafe of orange juice to pour herself a glass and Amir continued.

"When Sheena told me she was pregnant; it was on the same day I got offered my deal at Dope Records. She and I were arguing a lot in the months before that and we weren't getting along at all like we did when our relationship first started. So, the timing of the pregnancy was terrible."

"You two were still having sex enough for her to get pregnant so it couldn't have been that bad," Melodee said.

"Yeah, we were, but we still weren't on good terms." He exhaled. "When she told me she was pregnant, it was like my whole world stopped spinning. I wasn't ready to be a father. And I knew if I forced myself to be I wouldn't be a good one. You see how my dad wasn't around a lot? How it was just me and my mama?"

Melodee nodded.

"That would have been me, I already knew it. I would've been the part-time dad who kept my distance from my son. Pick him up on weekends, bring him to my place so he can experiment with my vinyl's, so that I could get caught up with the next woman in the room next door. No interaction. No conversation. I wouldn't be the father I wanted to be to a kid."

"But A.J., it was through that relationship that you found your calling."

"And that makes all of this bittersweet. I wanted more from my father, Mel. Yeah, his love of music inspired me to pursue a career in music but imagine how much more our relationship could have yielded if he was involved. I didn't want to be like that to a kid. So, when Sheena said she was pregnant, I was honest with her. I told her I didn't want to be a father. I had plans and having kids fresh out of high school wasn't one of them."

Melodee sighed heavy. "Okay, that's understandable. But after she did it, after she got rid of the baby, you weren't there. You weren't there for the procedure and you weren't there after she went through with it to care for her physically or emotionally."

"She didn't want me there, Mel. Sheena told me if she got the abortion, that was it for us."

"And you still let her go alone?" Melodee questioned. "That broke her, A.J. And now it's affected..." she paused. "She's just still not over it."

Amir exhaled. He interlocked his fingers together and placed his hands on top of his head and bit at his bottom lip. He sat quietly then said, "This is gonna sound real fucked up but the truth is, I never was into Sheena like that. She's a beautiful person inside and out but it was always you I wanted. But I figured okay, if Mel sees how good I am to her girl maybe she'd see that I could be as good to her, too. Maybe even better."

Melodee scoffed. "That is fucked up, A.J. Especially since you ended up dropping the ball by hurting her. Plus, I would never date my best friend's ex." It wasn't until after the words left her lips that she realized the hypocrisy in her words. Melodee dropped her head into her hands and blew raspberries with her lips. The reality of what she and Amir did the night before weighed heavy on her. Specifically, the reality of having to tell Sheena about it.

With her hands to her face, Amir coiled his arms around her waist and kissed her on her wrist.

"A.J., stop that."

He gently pulled her hand from her head and placed his finger on her chin to turn her head to look at him. Amir gave her that longing gaze once their eyes met. The same gaze that had her asking for more the night before. He leaned in closer and kissed her, brushing his lips against hers first before gliding his tongue into her mouth. Like the night before, the kiss was soulful, stopping time for Melodee, summoning her to submit, again. He kissed her with more than his lips. There was sensual energy in the caress of his tongue and the strength of his lips on hers. The moment they stopped kissing, she dropped her head.

"What did I get myself into?" she asked out loud to more so herself than to him.

He leaned in again and buried his nose and lips on her neck kissing her as she responded by moaning. His hands were on her thighs again when he whispered on her neck, "come here."

"I can't," she said in a whisper low voice. "I gotta go meet up with Sheena."

He swiveled the bar stool she sat on, turning her to face him. "Do that thing you did last night before you go."

Melodee couldn't help but to smile. "What thing is that?"

"You know what thing." Amir bit his lip. "That thing with your hips. It made me want to buy you an island... nah, a planet."

She laughed. "I don't have time for that. I have to go."

Amir wasn't trying to hear that and Melodee knew she wanted more. So, he stood up and walked between her thighs. He wrapped her legs around his waist to lift her up in his hands. She protested, demanding he put her down but not stern enough for him to obey. He carried her back up to his room and as requested, she did that thing with her hips that he loved so much. In return he did everything he noticed made her moan, and that she loved in bed the night before.

They made love again for over an hour as their hot breakfast turned cold.

Chapter Nine

Other than the humming sound the small radiator by the reception desk was making, the OBGYN's office where Melodee sat waiting for Sheena was quiet. She'd glanced down at her phone several times since arriving an hour earlier. It was after noon and her stomach was growling beneath her wool coat since she only ate a few bites at Amir's. Sheena was running over an hour late for her appointment and Melodee hoped everything was fine.

Around her sat pregnant women who rubbed their bellies, snacked on the complimentary pretzels, or read one of the pregnancy pamphlets sprawled out on the table beside them. The lights overhead were bright. Behind the reception area photos of babies delivered by the midwives and OBGYNs in the office laid tacked to a corkboard. Melodee smiled to herself. She pushed her hand into her coat's inside pocket to make sure her earring was still in there. Amir gave it back to her before she left with stern instructions to trash it or at least to never wear them again.

For no other reason besides nothing else to think about, her mind wandered to more thoughts of him. Remembering how his hands caressed her body, his fingers gliding up her skin making her shiver. She had to press her thighs close together when she recalled how he moved between her legs in sync with her movements, knowing what her body needed to ease her into a trance-like state.

"Mrs. Rincon?" the physician assistant dressed in floral scrubs called from the reception area.

Melodee looked down at her phone then toward the front door and sighed.

"Sheena Rincon?" the assistant called again.

Melodee stood to her feet and walked over to the assistant. They'd done this routine three times already that afternoon. "I'm sorry, she still isn't here yet."

The assistant pinched her lips together while tapping her acrylic nail against the top of Sheena's medical folder. "She'll need to reschedule her appointment. She's over an hour late."

"I know but—"

"Have Mrs. Rincon contact the office to reschedule when she's ready. We've had to push back several appointments already to accommodate her."

Melodee stepped out of the doctor's office and called Sheena. She'd avoided calling her earlier considering what happened the night before between her and Amir. She figured it would be best to go with Sheena to her appointment and that afterward, maybe, she would break the news about her and Amir. Keeping this from her best friend wasn't a choice at that point.

"Sheena, you're late for your appointment," Melodee said into her phone once Sheena answered.

"I'm not coming," Sheena replied. Her voice sounded shaky like she'd been crying.

"Why not?"

Sheena said nothing.

Melodee sighed. "Where are you?"

Melodee eyed her friend the moment she turned the corner onto Montague Street in Brooklyn Heights, seven blocks away from the OBGYN's office. Sheena was sitting at the window in a Haagen Dazs ice cream shop, shoveling chocolate ice cream into her mouth. Her shoulders were slumped and her gaze was entirely in the ice cream's cup even when she wasn't spooning more of the sweet treat into her mouth.

Sheena saw Melodee the moment she got in front of the shop and managed a half-smile and a wave. Melodee stepped into the shop, ordered a small cup of cookie dough ice cream, then joined her friend at her table.

Melodee and Sheena had been friends since their freshman years in high school. Sheena had just moved to New York from her hometown of Miami and knew no one, not even the neighborhood kids. The two befriended each other the first day of school in their Social Studies class. During the 13-years of their friendship, Melodee had learned the best way to deal with Sheena in her not-so-happy times. She knew Sheena hated questions when she was upset and that when she was ready, she'd talk about whatever was bothering her. So, Melodee sat across from her friend and spooned ice cream into her mouth, waiting.

Like always, Sheena started their conversation talking about things that had nothing to do with why she missed her appointment. She spoke about getting a new bag, about the new car she and Ray planned to get soon. Melodee smiled politely and nodded when necessary, still waiting for Sheena to tell her what was wrong.

"I'm tired of those damn appointments," Sheena finally said as she scrapped her spoon along the bottom of her ice cream cup. "The examinations, the blood work, only to be told that I'm still not pregnant. It's too much."

Melodee reached for her friend's hand and held it in her own. "I know, mama. But this is what you must do to get what you want, right?"

"Is it?" Tears slid down Sheena's cheek and Melodee pulled out a napkin from the napkin dispenser to blot Sheena's eyes. "I've been going to the doctor for the past six months, consistently getting the same news. It's to the point you are now coming with me and not Ray. He can't take it either. But he won't say that because he doesn't want to hurt my feelings."

Sheena's husband Ray took her miscarriage hard. He'd been excited when she told him the news two months before their wedding. She'd taken a home pregnancy test, and it showed positive. He found it to be perfect timing since they'd planned to start a family soon after the wedding, anyway. Although she was just a few weeks along, he'd already researched car seats and strollers. So, when he and Sheena went to the doctor for her first appointment and they couldn't find a heartbeat the news devastated them, especially Ray.

Sheena used her spoon to point at Melodee's half eaten ice cream and Melodee slid the cup over to her. Her appetite had been insane those past few months. And although Melodee wanted to say something about it she believed it would be too insensitive to point anything out.

"Ray doesn't ask me for much if for anything at all," Sheena confessed. "He gives me the world and I always feel like I'm constantly taking."

"That's not true."

Sheena's lip quivered and her eyes blinked back her tears. Melodee pushed her seat to Sheena's side and wrapped her arms around her best friend.

"The only thing he's ever asked me for was a baby, and I can't even give him that," she said through her tears. She sobbed onto Melodee's shoulder who held her tight in her arms.

The reality of everything weighed heavy on Melodee in that moment. Just hours before, the source of Sheena's pain was making Melodee reach climatic heights she never knew were possible. Her chest tightened as she held Sheena tighter, her friend finding it hard to control her tears, her sobs garnering attention from the other customers standing in line and sitting around them.

Melodee decided she wouldn't tell Sheena anything about her and Amir. How could she? Her eyes watered and she sniffed back tears of her own opting to stay strong for her girl.

But her tears were not only for Sheena. They were also for the reality of what Melodee needed to do. She had to end things with Amir before her feelings for him got too serious.

Chapter Ten

Before Melodee could knock on Amir's loft door, Big Ant slid it open. On his face was a wide smile and Melodee stared at him from the corner of her eye.

"What?" she asked with her hand on her hip.

"I'm just thrilled to see you." He gave her that all-knowing grin and based off that, she knew Amir told him what happened between the two of them.

How could Amir resist? Big Ant and Amir were as close as Melodee and Sheena, even closer since Ant now knew about Amir and Melodee's hookup while Sheena was still left in the dark.

"I'll meet y'all downstairs. He's up in his room," was all Ant said before stepping out and sliding the door closed behind Melodee.

The night before, Amir called Melodee to inform her he'd be in town for a club appearance and he wanted her to go with him. She would have declined especially considering Sheena's breakdown at the ice cream shop two days earlier, but Melodee figured it would be the perfect time to tell Amir they couldn't keep seeing each other.

Amir poked his head out of his room, looking down at his front door, and gave her that brilliant smile of his.

Melodee took a deep breath, pushing the air out through her lips.

"Come up. I want to show you something," he said stepping back into his room.

Melodee climbed the glass staircase headed for his room and when she got to his bedroom's door, her eyes were met with racks and racks of dresses. Some frilly, others sparkling. A few of them didn't even appear to be dresses at all, only strips of fabric. On his floor, lined against the wall, were a dozen variations of women's shoes, all designer name brand. Melodee didn't need to peek inside of the shoes to see that they were from expensive brands. The obvious scent from the leather linings and soles hinted that this was top shelf footwear.

"What is all of this?"

"It's all for you. I always get calls from designers and their reps who want to send me free clothes and shoes and figured I'd take advantage this time, but for you."

Melodee walked up to the racks and sifted through the clothes, sliding them from left to right on their hangers. Amir walked up behind her and wrapped his arms around her waist, placing a kiss on her neck. He tried to kiss her again on the same spot but she gently removed his arms and turned to face him.

He frowned. "You don't like them."

Melodee expelled a heavy sigh. "It's not that, A.J."

"You don't like me trying to dress you, right?" He ran his fingers through his curly top fade as he sat at the edge of his bed. "I meant no disrespect. I know how you independent women are. Your man was dying to give you something nice." He gave her wool sweater paired with blue jeans tucked into her brown riding boots a once-over. She'd gone straight home after work to change so that she didn't show up to his loft in her work attire.

"You can wear what you got on. I always dug your style, so it's whatever."

She looked at him and the way his body had a natural sheen that glowed underneath his overhead lights. How everything about him was perfect from his complexion to the shape of his brows. It was impossible to shake the thoughts of him making love to her right on the bed he now sat on looking up at her.

Noticing her gawk, he licked his lips and curved his finger, gesturing for her to come to him. She smiled, shaking her head. She told herself she wouldn't sleep with him tonight. So, if going to the club with him will get them away from a bed long enough for her to tell him they couldn't see each other anymore, so be it.

Melodee turned to face the rack of clothes again and picked out a simple black Versace dress with a high split at the side. She turned the dress around to get a better view, pressing the sleek black dress against her body while looking at herself in Amir's full-length mirror.

"I'll wear this one," she said. She pointed at a pair of silver sandals that sparkled from the bevy of clustered Swarovski crystals that covered every part including the straps that tied above the ankles. "And I'll wear those."

When they arrived in front of Club 69, the black suited chauffeur pulled open the door of Amir's Maybach to throngs of screaming fans, most of which were scantily clad women with the top of their breasts exposed in below thirty-degree weather. Amir stepped out dressed in a black designer pea coat with velvet loafers. Under his coat, he wore a crisp white dress shirt, with the buttons unbuttoned near his neck, paired with tailored slacks. He was always red carpet ready at every event. Never wearing jeans or sweatpants outside of his loft.

Amir reached for Melodee's hand, and she grabbed his tightly as she followed close behind him. Before leaving the loft, Amir insisted that Melodee wear a cropped pure white fur coat along with Tom Ford cat-eyed shades that were sent to him. Though it was winter and her bare legs would be exposed, the fur coat she could understand. But she found it ridiculous to wear sunglasses at night. After stepping out of the car and seeing the sea of cameras flashing in front of them, Amir's suggestion made sense. Without the sunglasses, Melodee would have been blinded by the flashing camera bulbs. Amir had gotten used to it.

He smiled and waved at the crowd of fans and paparazzi as they entered the club, his hand still holding Melodee's.

"You all right?" he asked over the commotion.

Melodee nodded but inside she was petrified. Her heart was beating a mile a minute. All eyes were on her. Some looking in awe, others with envy. There were so many questions being yelled out by the people holding cameras.

"Amir, who's your girl?"

"Are you off the market?"

"Is that your new girlfriend?"

He ignored them all, wrapping his arms briefly around Melodee and giving her a kiss on her cheek to send the message without having to say a word.

Club 69 was packed to the brim with people. This was odd to Melodee since it was a Tuesday night.

"Don't these people work?" Melodee asked in Amir's ear so he could hear her over the loud pumping music.

"This is work, love," he replied.

Bottle girls walked through the club with sparklers poking out the necks of champagne bottles on their way to VIP. People on the dance floor moved rhythmically to the songs the DJ spun.

When Amir walked in, the MC announced his arrival and the crowd went wild. Amir took the mic, said a few words including that his new album Black Rose was dropping soon and smiled for a few pictures before walking up to VIP with Melodee.

They sat on a lounge chair with a select number of people sipping on champagne, wines, and spirits.

Melodee downed her champagne quick hoping it would calm her nerves. Her mind was scrambled with questions, one being what was taking her so long to tell Amir she couldn't see him anymore.

Amir hadn't let Melodee's hand go since they stepped out of the Maybach. She found his protectiveness over her to be real sweet. Every so often he'd lean over and give her a kiss on the cheek or neck to let her know that even though people were pulling his attention in all different directions, that he was still thinking of her. For most of the night, he was drawn into conversations and quick interviews with artists, executives, or journalists whose primary reason for being at the club that night was to see and talk to Amir.

With his attention elsewhere, Melodee leaned back on the couch and sipped on her champagne. She scanned the faces of everyone in the VIP room, which weren't many. There were a handful of guys, but the women outnumbered them all. One woman dressed in a tight hot pink bandeau dress kept eyeing Melodee from her seat at the private VIP bar. Melodee thought it was all in her head when she caught the woman staring, but she brushed it off.

Melodee was in her own world when the woman finally worked up the gall to walk over to Melodee and sit beside her.

The woman pushed her bare legs real close to Melodee's getting her attention. When Melodee turned to glare at the woman, that same woman glided her tongue along the bottom of her top lip, seductively slow.

"Hey, I'm Kandi," she said into Melodee's ear.

Melodee leaned away and scooted a little closer to Amir whose attention was on the conversation he was having with the person to his right.

Melodee replied with a, "Hi Kandi."

"So, you're Amir's girl, right? I figured you were since he's been holding your hand the whole time he's been here," Kandi said gesturing to their interlocked fingers.

"Something like that," Melodee said.

"Hmph," Kandi countered taking a sip of her drink through a skinny red straw. "Well, I came over here to tell you that I'm down to join y'all tonight if you are."

Melodee gave her an incredulous stare. She wasn't sure if she'd heard Kandi right. The music was loud, and the champagne was making her head light. "I'm sorry?"

"A threesome. You, me, and Amir," Kandi replied matter-of-factly. As if she were suggesting they have dinner and not sex. She glanced up and Melodee looked in the direction Kandi was looking. There were three other ladies by the bar whose attentions were on Melodee and Kandi.

"I'd already planned to fuck Amir tonight," Kandi added, "but since he's here with you and the two of you are whatever y'all are, I thought I'd be kind enough to ask you if you'd like to share him tonight instead of stepping on your toes to get to him."

A heavy feeling in Melodee's stomach kept her from responding. The room moved to the beat of the song playing throughout the club as she got dizzy.

Melodee looked over at Amir who was still busy talking then back at Kandi and said, "We'll pass, thank you."

Kandi kissed her teeth. She stretched her slim arm over Melodee to rub Amir's knee with her palm. He leaned over to see Kandi waving, and he gave her a polite nod and smile then went right back to his conversation.

Melodee clenched her jaw and gave Kandi a sullen glare. Kandi grinned in response.

"The truth is," Kandi told Melodee, "I was just being nice when I extended an invitation to you. I've already decided to fuck your man tonight, so that's what I'll do regardless of how you feel about it."

Melodee's jaw dropped as the words left Kandi's lips. She looked around the room wondering if this exchange was happening in real life. Her chest burned and her free hand balled into a fist. Realizing where her temper and Kandi were pushing her to do, she pulled her hand free from Amir's and stood to her feet.

Amir ended his conversation immediately and looked up at Melodee. "What's up?"

"I gotta go," Melodee replied looking down to her left at Kandi who was looking over at Amir, trying to give him the sexiest stare she could to get his attention.

"Okay," Amir said standing up and gesturing to Big Ant, "I'll go with you."

"No, you stay. It's your party."

"I've already gotten paid and fulfilled my obligation. I could've left after that." He took her hand so they could walk out. "Come on and let's go."

"Hey, Amir," Kandi called desperately from behind Melodee and Amir as they walked away.

She tried to walk up behind them but Big Ant stepped right in her path blocking her. "He's leaving. Have a seat."

Amir and Melodee were making their way toward the VIP exit when Melodee looked over her shoulder to glance at Kandi with narrowed eyes. Melodee couldn't hear her but she read Kandi's lips when she mouthed, "that bitch."

Amir and Melodee were outside of the club when about twenty fans surrounded the Maybach begging for pictures and autographs. Big Ant and two other bodyguards kept a few more fans away from the car as Amir happily smiled for cameras, took selfies with eager fans, and signed autographs. Women poked out their breasts with Sharpees in hand requesting he sign his name on their cleavage.

Melodee sat in the car with her arms folded in front of her chest, her lips set in a pout. She was red hot after what happened in the club minutes ago. She'd never experienced that kind of anger before that night. Jealousy was foreign to her but very familiar in that moment with Kandi. Kandi's audacity and sureness in getting her way shocked Melodee to her core and left her feeling a little insecure.

She and Amir were outside of the club for about ten minutes when Amir said the last of his goodbyes and joined her in the Maybach. He turned in his seat to see Melodee's arms folded tight over her breasts, her crossed legs fidgeting as she sat in her seat.

"I apologize, Mel," he said leaning over to kiss her on the cheek. "I'm all yours now." With her arms still folded, his hand pushed past her cropped fur coat in search of her breasts to caress.

She leaned away from him in her seat, her eyes still facing forward.

"Uh-oh. What did I do, now?"

Melodee looked at him from the side of her eye. "You saw that woman who was sitting next to me in VIP with the pink dress on?"

"The pretty redbone? Yeah, I saw her."

She turned her head to him and looked at him with narrowed eyes. "You thought she was pretty?"

"Um, I..." he stammered, his eyes on hers, trying to read her, hoping her expression would help him answer the question in a way that wouldn't piss her off even more.

Melodee scoffed loudly. "You know what she asked me? She asked if she could join us for a threesome, tonight."

Amir snorted.

"Oh, that's funny to you?"

Her reaction turned his snort to boisterous laughter. He poked her on her side and said, "Come on, you have to admit it's a little funny."

Melodee rolled her eyes at him.

"Aw, I'm sorry, Mel," he said kissing her on her cheek again. "You see who I left with, right? Besides, she must've thought you were bad if she wanted you, too."

"Oh no, she was being polite when she invited me."

She looked away and drew back the curtain covering the window to look out at the street as the chauffeur drove them. They were passing by the back streets of Time Square where all the porn DVD shops, strip clubs, and peepshows laid hidden in the shadows of the iconic location.

"A.J.?" she muttered. Her attention still on the passing shops.

"Yeah, Mel?"

"How many threesomes have you had?"

"Seriously?"

She turned to him. "Yes, seriously. How many have you had?"

Amir's eyes pointed upward at the roof of the car as he stroked the trimmed hairs of his goatee with his fingers. His brows wrinkled as he thought hard. He was quiet, using his fingers on both hands to count. "This year or last year?"

Melodee gasped, and this made him laugh.

"This year I've had none because you've been my focus since December. But last year is tough to recall."

"Are you kidding me?"

"What, Mel? Come on now." He nudged her like a friend would do to another friend who was tripping.

Melodee sat up in her seat and stared at him. "Oh. My. God. How many women have you slept with... like up until now and including me?"

"To be honest, I lost count. But I make sure to always get tested even though I use condoms every time," he insisted.

"You really don't know how many?" She probed. "How about 10? 20? 30?"

Amir shrugged.

"More than 30?!"

"Definitely more than 30."

Melodee shook her head and dropped herself back against her seat. "The ménage twins at your party warned me about you and your threesomes. How one girl was never enough for you."

Amir objected. "Don't believe everything you hear, okay?"

"Well, do you? Enjoy having threesomes?"

Amir turned to face her completely. "I did... when I had them. I loved it. Two women competing for my attention in bed, waiting and wanting me to fuck them even knowing I fucked the woman to her left. Every man loves having options especially in bed, Mel. And if a brother ever tells you otherwise he's lying."

Melodee sighed.

"But you're enough for me," he said. He placed his finger on her chin, turning her face so her eyes could meet with his as he spoke from the heart. "I already told you I was over that life. I don't want the redbone in the tight pink dress. I want the brown skin queen in the classy black dress. I want me a Melodee." He smiled then licked his lips. "A smart woman with a fat ass that she keeps covered and only lets me see when we're alone."

She tried to fight back the smile pulling at her lips.

"A woman who has her own goals, independent of me." He kissed the back of her hand. "And who'll tell me, *I don't want your money, A.J.*," he said in his best impression of her in his attempt to impersonate what she told him at his loft the night they made love.

"I love how I don't have to worry about us being intimate at night and the world hearing about it in the morning. Plus, you the homie and my mama loved you! Yeah, you're not only who I want, you're who I need. So best believe that's enough for me."

He brushed his lips against hers, his hand moving up her leg sliding between the split in her dress. "Comfort over chaos, love, that's what I'm all about now."

"Are you sure?"

"One thousand percent sure."

Amir used the tip of his tongue to tease her top lip and this made her smile. He pushed the button to bring the partition up in front of them to separate them from the driver.

"The way you wrap around me when I'm inside of you feels too damn good and too damn real for me to want anyone other than you."

His fingers moved between her thighs and she slid her legs apart to make his journey easier.

"Mmm." She moaned when his fingers found her sweet spot behind her panties. She pressed her head against the headrest of her seat and looked over at him, smiling then biting her lip.

"This right here to me, is like the rarest treasure on the planet," he whispered. Amir brought his mouth to her neck to suck on the space above her collarbone while stroking the pink nub between her thighs with his finger. She arched her back when he pushed that same finger inside of her, meeting his finger thrusts by jutting her hip forward.

"Why the hell would I ever want to share you with anybody?" He groaned as her juices coated his fingertip.

Their eyes were on each other when Melodee glided the pad of her thumb along the fullest part of his bottom lip.

"This is so wrong," she whispered.

He pressed his lips against her finger, kissing all her fingertips, one at a time.

"Nah, it's just right." He grabbed her chin and brushed his lips against hers and she let her tongue entwine with his when he kissed her.

Amir's driver pulled the Maybach over by the curb in front of Amir's loft and Melodee stepped out with Amir, following him up to his place with no hesitation.

In the back of her mind, she knew she'd eventually have to end things with Amir. Sheena finding out about them would be too devastating of a truth for their friendship to survive.

But that night, Melodee craved the one thing Kandi and all the other groupies of America desired but couldn't have anymore, Amir's attention.

Chapter Eleven

A rush of cold winter air pushed behind Melodee as she entered the building of Dr. Sherida Pierce's private office. Melodee immediately sighed at the relief of warm air that bathe her skin the moment she walked into the lobby of the building. Like routine, she smiled politely at security, pressed the elevator call button, and rode the elevator to the 5th floor. She unlocked the doors of the office and dropped her belongings down onto her desk.

She was blushing with thoughts of Amir but every time she felt herself about to smile about their newfound connection, she quickly frowned, realizing she still hadn't told Sheena. Normally, Sheena was the first person to hear about anything great going on in Melodee's life. The moment she got engaged, Sheena was the first to know. After she and her ex-husband Jaden bought their new condo, Sheena got the phone call about it the moment they got the keys. Now that Melodee had found someone who helped take the sting out of her divorce, someone Sheena already knew, she couldn't share it because of Sheena and Amir's history.

She dropped herself on her chair and slouched her shoulders. Melodee kept telling herself that she'd end things with Amir today but there had been several todays. After seeing him that Tuesday night, she swore she'd tell him they couldn't see each other, the next morning. But Wednesday and Thursday came and went, and still she hadn't done it.

Now it was a Friday. There was only one day left in January. That made it over a month of Amir and Melodee secretly seeing each other behind Sheena's back. The idea alone made Melodee sick to her stomach.

Things slowed down in Dr. Sherida Pierce's office around 2 p.m. This was the usual as most of Sherida's clients didn't like coming in to see her on Fridays. Who wants to discuss their marriage and the problems in it on the happiest day of the week? So, Melodee buried her nose in one of her psychology textbooks.

Until the office phone rang.

"Dr. Sherida Pierce's office."

"Come see me in Jamaica, tonight," Amir said on the other end of the phone.

Melodee pushed her chair back and ducked her head underneath her desk. "What?" she whispered into the phone.

"Jamaica," he repeated. "My last show is in Montego Bay tonight and I want you to be there."

"A.J., didn't I tell you not to call me here?"

"I know, but you weren't answering your cell."

Melodee looked up from her desk to make sure Sherida wasn't hearing her.

Every time the phone rang, it was as if Sherida was conditioned to listen in, waiting for Melodee to transfer the call. Melodee understood why that was though. She knew that Sherida's practice was private. Meaning she was responsible for getting and keeping her paying clients. So, every time the phone rang, it was like hearing a cash register drawer slide open. If Melodee didn't tell Sherida she had a call or that a client was confirming their appointment, Sherida got suspicious.

"That's because I'm at work," she answered Amir. "You know that thing people do when they aren't getting paid one hundred-thousand dollars just to say ten or less words into a microphone in a club."

He chuckled. "Was that shade?"

"Melodee?" Sherida called from her office.

Melodee sighed heavy. "I gotta go, A.J."

"Just say yes."

"How am I supposed to get to Jamaica, tonight? How long is the flight?"

"Three-and-a-half hours. I can charter a plane for you to get down here. It'll be ready to go whenever you are."

"You're already there?" she asked.

"Melodee?! That have better not be a personal call," Sherida yelled from her office.

"Yup," Amir said, pulling Melodee's attention back. "I just walked out of my villa and onto my private beach overlooking the water. You'd love it. It's about eighty-degrees down here, Mel. The sun is out, sand is crystal white and warm. Only thing missing on this beautiful island is you. So, escape the cold for the weekend, baby. Only for one night."

Melodee bit inside of her cheek and considered the idea. It was freezing in New York, about twenty degrees but it felt below zero. Her toes had finally defrosted enough for her to wiggle them after warming up next to the corner radiator she had beside her desk.

"Just come as you are. Don't worry about going home first. I got everything covered. I'll have my driver pick you up and bring you to Teterboro Airport for your flight. All you gotta do is say yes."

"Melodee," Sherida said, poking her head out of her office door. When she saw Melodee leaning forward in her chair with her head underneath her desk with the phone, she stepped completely out of her office.

"Okay, yes," she blurted. "Tell him to be here around 5 p.m."

Before Amir could respond, Melodee stood to her feet to place the phone down on its port to end the call.

Sherida stood in front of Melodee's desk with her hand on her waist. She stared at Melodee with a pinched expression. With her jaw clenched she asked, "was that a personal call?"

Melodee looked her right in the eyes and replied, "No, it was one of your clients confirming their appointment."

"Which one?" Sherida countered, her face tightening.

Melodee managed a hard smile. "Your next one."

Sherida sighed loud, turning to walk away while shaking her head, visibly annoyed.

Melodee paid her no mind. Usually she would have rolled her eyes and fell back in her chair waiting impatiently to get out of there, anticipating running home to dive face first into a tub of chocolate ice cream. But she was getting something better than chocolate ice cream that night. In a few hours, she'd be in Jamaica, with Amir.

As instructed, Amir's driver was in front of Sherida's office building at 5 p.m. on the dot. She stood up from her desk and pressed the call button for the elevator while cuing up her favorite podcast, Lamar At Knight, on her phone, quickly plugging her ears.

Both Melodee and Sherida rode the elevator down together, not Melodee's choice, and when they walked through the turning doors, Sherida took notice of the Maybach that stood out like a gem in a line of parked black SUVs.

"Hmm, he must be here for someone important," Sherida said gesturing at Amir's chauffeur standing at the driver's side of the Maybach. Her eyes along with most of the people passing by were on the sleek white Maybach parked out front. The moment the black-suited driver saw Melodee, he hurried around to the car's backdoor closest to Melodee.

"Good afternoon, Melodee," he said pulling open the back door of the Maybach, "Your flight is scheduled to leave in 20-minutes so we should get going right away."

Melodee turned to Sherida whose jaw was now hanging open and said, "See you on Monday, Dr. Pierce."

Melodee placed the strap of her brown leather satchel over her head and down to her shoulders then flipped her curls over her shoulder while walking away. She thanked the driver, and got into the Maybach, watching Sherida through the side of her eye as the chauffeur closed her door. Sherida just stood there staring, confused and trying to understand how her receptionist had a chauffeur while she was still taking public transportation to and from the office.

Right before the chauffeur drove off, Melodee smiled at Sherida's gawk then closed the curtain on her side of the window, giggling to herself.

The flight from New York to Montego Bay, Jamaica was a dream for Melodee. The moment she stepped onto Amir's chartered private plane, she was greeted with a glass of bubbly champagne by one of the two black flight attendants. These women were beautiful and looked runway ready with their long legs, form-fitting blue skirt suits, and bright smiles.

Melodee sat back in the buttery brown leather plane seat, the cushion of the seat molding to her bottom immediately. She pulled her phone out of her satchel and turned it off then unzipped her boots, freed her feet, and kicked them up as she reclined back, taking a relaxing deep breath.

Soon after stepping on to the plane, the pilot walked to the back of the cabin to where Melodee was to introduce himself. After they exchanged pleasantries he said, "We should be in Montego Bay by 9 p.m., Ms. Delon. If you need anything, please don't hesitate to ask your flight attendants, Judie and Shania. Mr. Jones insisted that we take great care of you during your flight."

With those words spoken he excused himself and moments later they were up in the air.

The steady sounds of the engines during the flight were so soothing, Melodee fell asleep two hours into the flight. She was awoken by the wheels of the plane touching down on the tarmac and the plane softly braking to a stop.

Heat was the first thing to touch her face as she stepped down the plane's stairs still wearing her sweater dress and boots from work. She felt overdressed as she passed women with tiny bikini tops and rayon sarongs wrapped around their waists clutching tour guide pamphlets in their hands while greeting new arrivals outside the airport.

Melodee was ushered to a black car where she got in and turned to face the window. She shook her head in disbelief. It was impossible for her to believe that just three hours earlier she was sitting at her desk in cold New York.

The sun had already set by the time Melodee arrived, but the warmth of Jamaica was all she needed. In the night, as her car rolled by headed to Amir's villa, she could see the goats along the road nibbling on stalks of grass. In the distance behind them, were the beautiful homes set on hills and painted in a variety of tropical colors. Palm trees led the way as people jerked and grilled chicken and other meats on the side of the road outside small restaurants for waiting customers.

Melodee rolled the window down to breathe in the air that smelled different from the air in New York. It was fresher. Crisper.

She was taken to a private beach where Amir was staying and escorted to Amir's villa.

"Mr. Jones told us to tell you that a driver will be here by 10 p.m. to pick you up," the 30-something butler said with his thick Jamaican accent.

Melodee pulled off her boots the moment she walked into the villa. She brought her hands to her lips and swooned when she saw the bouquet of pink roses from Amir to her sitting on the front table near the entrance with her name on a card in front of it. The villa was huge and very spacious complete with five bedrooms, five-and-a-half bathrooms, a large master's bedroom with doors that opened out on to the beach. As she walked around the space, her jaw dropped even more as she toured the amenities. When she stepped outside, the infinity pool and outdoor shower made her gasp then scream with elation. The view was breathtaking. She brought her hand to her chest, her fingers spreading out against her breastbone in awe. She stepped out onto the beach and the white sand sunk beneath her toes as she watched the ocean water move and sparkle beneath the natural glow of the moon.

Back inside, in the master bedroom, a large sheer white curtain hung from the ceiling and draped over the bed framed by a gold canopy. Except for the bed and dresser, the rest of the furniture were made with high quality wicker.

The bathroom was massive with double sinks, a stand-in shower with multiple shower heads and a hot tub in front of an open window that offered another view of the beach.

Lying on the bed, was a simple plain white maxi dress and on the floor, flat metallic Manolo Blahnik sandals. Melodee smiled to herself pleased to see that Amir had already learned her style.

She hopped in the shower to wash off the day then primped herself the best she could in the bathroom's mirror. Melodee pulled her hair up into a bun, securing it with two rubber bands she found on the bedroom's nightstand then wiggled herself into the white maxi dress. The dress fit perfectly, hugging her curves, stressing her hourglass figure.

Soon she was in the back of the black car again, whizzing down the paved Jamaican road with sounds of Bob Marley playing from the car's radio.

When they arrived at the venue, that was outside and overlooked the beach, Big Ant met her at the entrance.

"Finally," he said pressing his palms together. "You know he's been asking everybody and their mama if you've arrived, right? He hasn't been able to talk about anything else."

Melodee grinned as they walked through the underpass of the venue, passing by security and throngs of fans waiting to get in to watch the show.

"He refused to go out on stage until he saw you first," Big Ant continued. He towered over her so Melodee had to crane her neck to look up at him to make eye contact. "I don't know what you're doing to him but you're making him really happy." He leaned back behind her and said, "Must be how that booty's poking out in that dress."

Melodee pinched his arm. "You better stop before I call Shanice and tell her you're over here looking at other women's booties in Jamaica," she said referring to his wife.

"Woman, I'm married not blind."

They turned the corner headed to Amir's dressing room when Amir stepped out the door followed by his team and entourage. The moment he and Melodee's eyes met they smiled big at each other.

His publicist, Denise, a petite middle-aged woman with salt-and-pepper colored hair and who Amir referred to as his mama number two, was going over her checklist, telling him the plans for the next day which included an interview with a journalist from a local Jamaican newspaper, Jamaica Daily. Denise resembled Dionne Warwick and had the raspy voice to match.

Amir had stopped listening to Denise speak the moment he saw Melodee. The world turned mute around them as they looked at each other. In his signature, unbuttoned dress shirt with the sleeves rolled up, untied bow tie, black slacks, and designer loafers, Melodee removed it all as she ripped them off him with her eyes. Amir's view traveled over the curves in her breasts and hips wetting his lips in anticipation of getting her alone.

In the middle of Denise speaking he walked away from her and toward Melodee. When he was close enough, he took Melodee's hand and interlocked his fingers with hers. He placed his other hand on the curve of her lower back and pressed her body closer to him.

"Hi," he whispered on her lips.

"Hey," she said back. She pressed her palm against his cheek then brushed her lips against his. With no hesitation or regard for the people standing around them they kissed, passionately, his hand caressing her back her palm stroking his cheek as their tongues glided against one another and made love inside their mouths. After what felt like forever for everyone else but just a few seconds to them, they broke their kiss and smiled at each other.

"Well, damn," Denise exclaimed while fanning herself. "I'm gonna need to call my husband and take a cold shower after seeing that."

The hallway erupted in laughter as Melodee and Amir laughed too, still looking at each other giving one another that all-knowing seductive stare.

Amir's tour manager stepped forward and said, "I hate to interrupt, but you gotta get on stage, Amir."

Amir gave Melodee a peck on the lips and said, "Be right back. Let me go make this money," before smiling and walking toward the stage.

The band cued up the music and the moment Amir stepped out, the fans screamed at the top of their lungs. Some chanted his name, others were just screaming, all of them excited to see him live and in-person.

Melodee stood backstage watching him, her heart feeling full and her face hurting from smiling so much. There must have been over ten thousand people in the audience but all she could see from her view was Amir.

For the next hour, Amir's soulful voice echoed and filled the outside space as he sang songs off his past albums and three songs from his new one, Black Rose, including his hit "Paper Thorns."

Halfway through his set, he looked to his left where Melodee was standing backstage and said into the microphone, "can I sing something to you?"

The audience screamed yes, believing he was talking to them but everyone realized backstage who he was really asking.

Melodee nodded slowly.

He walked toward his band to pick up his acoustic guitar. A stagehand brought a chair on stage which Amir sat on. As he adjusted his mic and strummed his guitar, the crowd went wild.

Melodee caressed her chest imagining it was his hands on her, finding it incredibly sexy how he had the audience wrapped around his pinky, waiting with bated breath for him to just sing.

"This is a song I added last minute to my new album after spending time with someone special," he said to the screaming audience. "It's a remake of Al Green's 'Simply Beautiful' a song that describes this angel perfectly. Y'all ready?"

"If I gave you my love," he sang. *"I'd tell you what I'd do."*

The crowd swooned and moved to his voice as his guitar filled the space of the outside arena acoustically grabbing hold of hearts and leaving them panting for more once the song was done.

He looked over at Melodee again and sat quiet for a moment giving her a yearning look. The audience roared in the background replacing his silence. Melodee leaned her head against the sidewall just staring back, biting her bottom lip.

"Can I admit something to you, Jamaica?" he asked turning his gaze to the audience before looking back at Melodee. The crowd welcomed whatever he had to say or give and showed their approval by screaming.

He ran his fingers through his curly top fade then said, "I'm so in love."

Melodee's jaw dropped and her eyes widened as a chorus of gasps and *awes* could be heard over her shoulder backstage. When she turned around to look at Big Ant, he mouthed, "Whoa!"

Melodee brought her fingers to her lips as she turned to look back in Amir's direction. The crowd erupted with loud applause while Melodee's heart felt like it was about to burst.

"Sheena's gonna kill me," Melodee said under her breath.

Chapter Twelve

After signing autographs, smiling for pictures, and meeting with winners who won tickets to Abacus and Amir's final show, Amir and Melodee were finally back at his villa alone.

They lounged on the private beach, feet away from his luxurious villa. Melodee sat between Amir's legs, leaning back against his chest. Amir rolled up a joint because really, they couldn't be in Jamaica and not sample the island's green. They passed the rolled up joint back and forth to each other. The two were silent, listening to the sounds of Jamaica's nature. Outside was dark with light only being provided by tiki torches, the thick stems of the tall fiery sticks buried deep in the sand. The sound of the ocean water washing over the sand and drenching the granular surface, was calming and heightened by their high.

"Look up," Amir told Melodee.

When she gazed up at the stars, she smiled.

"I think they're only extinct in New York."

Melodee giggled, her eyes still pointing up at the sky. There were so many stars in the sky, the glints of light from the tiny luminous spheres above reflected on the moving blanket of water in front of them.

Amir took Melodee's left hand into his and he slid his fingers down to the webbing of her fingers. He singled out her ring finger. "I wanna put something here one day."

Melodee sighed in discomfort before leaning forward and away from Amir. Her eyes were now on the sand below them as she scooped it up in her hollowed hand and watched it sift through her fingers.

"Uh-oh," he said leaning to his left to get a better view of her. "I said something wrong again."

Melodee glanced over her shoulder at him and shook her head. "You always say the right things."

"So, what was that?"

She dusted the sand from her hands. "It's nothing." She was quiet. "It's just that I don't know if I'd want to do that again."

Amir sat up straight. "Because of your divorce?"

Melodee pushed the air she inhaled out of her mouth.

"Mel, please don't hold me accountable for your ex-husband's actions. He was stupid and didn't appreciate the good woman he had. But I see your worth. I already told you I would never do that to you."

She kept her back facing him when she said, "I understand that, but I'm not sure if that's a route I'd like to take again. My wedding was so big. I invited everybody. It was a huge deal. Getting married and doing all of that, again... I'm just not sure."

"Can you look at me, please?" he asked, gently turning her by the shoulder so she could face him.

When she turned around, slowly bringing her eyes to meet his, he studied her. His hand was on her chin when she closed her eyes and pressed her cheek into his palm.

"For me, it's always been you. These feelings I have for you aren't new. The only difference is they're stronger now and realer. You've never let me in like you're doing now so I want to take full advantage." Amir couldn't help the smile pushing his cheeks back. "I don't want to keep things the same between us. I'm going to eventually want to give you more."

Melodee sighed.

He snorted. "Damn Mel, I'm not saying I want to marry you tomorrow." He tried to poke her on her side like he always did, but this time she playfully swatted his hand away and grinned at him.

"Oh yeah?" he teased, leaning closer to her and tickling her instead.

She giggled at his touch, trying her best to push his hand off but couldn't so she pushed her weight on to him, knocking Amir down to his back.

Laughing, the two tousled and rolled around as they wrestled in the sand. Amir exalted his dominance by pinning her down by her wrists the moment he got the chance. He released her to lean forward and brush his nose against hers, kissing her from her cheek to her ear.

He whispered, "You know I love you, right?"

She dusted sand from his hair, smoothing her hands down to his cheeks then running her finger across the rind of his bottom lip as he hovered over staring down at her. She scanned his face to see if the words he said matched the gleam in his eyes. It did. Her hand caressed his lip once more before she clasped her wrists behind his head and she said, "I love you too," before pulling him into a kiss.

The next morning, around 8 a.m., two hours before Amir and Melodee had to board the private plane back to New York, they sat in a Montego Bay restaurant for breakfast and an interview. Pelican Grill was a nice sized eatery with scents of seafood, jerked chicken, and pork salting the air. The soft brown leather booths, wooden tables, and chairs added sophistication to the atmosphere while the plants gave it that authentic Caribbean charm.

Amir, Melodee, and Jamaica Daily journalist, Courtney Sims, sat in a booth near the back of the restaurant. She was a blonde haired, blue eyed woman who had an all-American girl style but the voice of a Jamaican native. Over a breakfast of Jamaican callaloo and saltfish complete with green banana and dumpling, Amir answered questions for the local paper.

"I'm gonna ask you the one question everyone wants me to ask: do you have a release date for Black Rose, yet?" Courtney queried.

"Not yet," Amir replied.

"You seem to be keeping the release date to yourself. Is it somewhat of a secret?"

"I don't want to announce a date and feel pressured to get the album out by that time. That would lead to the songs sounding rushed and not well thought out or recorded. I couldn't do that to my fans... release subpar material. I'll announce a date when I'm confident it's ready."

Throughout the interview, when Courtney would ask Amir questions, she'd glance over at Melodee who would only smile back.

Before the interview started, Melodee told Amir she'd sit at another table to give them privacy but he insisted she stay by his side.

"Makes sense," Courtney said, again stealing a glance at Melodee. "I'd be a bad journalist if I didn't ask who your lady friend here is."

Amir and Melodee glanced at each other. He looked at Courtney. "She's someone special."

"Your girlfriend?"

Amir turned his chin to his shoulder in Denise's direction who was sitting at the table beside them and she immediately interjected. "That's gonna be a no comment for now."

For most of Amir's career, he's always aimed to keep his relationships private since most of his life is an open book. It's usually the women he dates who are the ones to advertise their relationship to anyone who will listen or pay for them to talk. Also, per Denise, giving the public the illusion that he was a single man was best for his career versus everyone viewing him as tied down to someone.

Courtney reached for her silver recorder laying on the table and pressed the red record button to stop recording. She turned to Denise and tried to bargain with her. "What if I keep it off the record?"

Denise replied, "No comment on or off the record, Courtney."

Courtney nodded then smiled at Melodee. "Are you an actress or model?"

Melodee shook her head. "No."

Courtney kept her eyes on Melodee as if she were expecting Melodee to add something else. This wasn't surprising to Melodee. She understood everyone wondered who the girl Amir kept close by his side was and what she did. So, Melodee said, "I'm just a regular girl from Brooklyn."

Courtney smiled.

Melodee looked away shyly. When she glanced over to her far left past Denise, Amir's assistant was holding his cellphone up in his hand. He saw her looking and smiled at her while quickly putting the phone away.

"She's being modest." Amir turned to Melodee and she directed her attention back on him. He grabbed her hand beneath the table and she interlocked her fingers with his. "She's my muse."

"Your muse?"

"Yeah, always has been," he replied. Amir and Melodee were still looking in each other's eyes when he squeezed her hand beneath the table, licking his lips and making her blush. "She's the reason I recorded a remake of 'Simply Beautiful.' She's inspired me to write and record two new songs for a new album."

Melodee's eyebrows arched, a big smile pulling at the side of her lips.

In that moment, Amir and Melodee were lost in each other's gazes, again. Denise cleared her throat, drawing their attention to her. She gave them a stern stare like a parent glaring at her kids in the rearview mirror from the front seat as they misbehaved in the back.

"Okay, this thing you're doing is extremely sexy," Courtney said.

They both glanced at her with wrinkled brows.

"The way you two look at each other like there's no one else in the room," Courtney added. "Your lady fans will lose their minds when they find out you're in love, Mr. Jones."

Melodee swallowed hard. She clasped the glass with her rum punch, brought it to her lips, and chugged it until the glass was empty. She knew there was one lady in particular who would lose her mind and probably more. And her name is Sheena.

As Melodee swallowed the spiked punch, feeling it as it moved down her throat and into her belly, she promised herself she'd tell Sheena about her evolved friendship with Amir the moment she touched down in New York.

Chapter Thirteen

A blizzard hit New York City that same Saturday Amir and Melodee were supposed to return. The storm dropped up to four feet of wind-driven snow on the city, crippling travel via railways, roadways, and air. So instead of traveling from Jamaica, they hung back for an extra day and flew in to New York during the early morning hours on Sunday. They made the most out of their extra day stay. He chased her around the villa and his private beach naked, making love to her after catching her in his arms. For the rest of that night they laid in each other's arms in the nude. They reminisced about old times while blowing smoke clouds overhead, enjoying the only threesome Melodee would allow, with Mary Jane.

On their way back to New York, Amir insisted that Melodee come to his loft. He said he had something special there for her to see but Melodee told him she needed to go home to study. That wasn't the entire truth. Melodee had studying to do, true, but she hadn't spoken to Sheena in two days and this was unlike her. Because of roaming charges, Melodee turned off her phone the moment she boarded her flight to Jamaica and hadn't turned it back on until she was back in her condo. Lying about being absent for two days was one thing, but three days of being MIA would seem suspicious. She and Sheena spent most of their weekends together so there was no doubt Sheena was trying to get in touch with her to find out where she was all weekend.

It was after 4 p.m. when Melodee finally got settled. She sat on her couch, folded her legs, and slid open her phone. She had ten missed phone calls and two text messages, all from Sheena.

Sheena didn't leave a single voicemail and her text messages consisted of *where are you?* and *call me.*

Melodee highlighted Sheena's number and before she could click it to call her, her doorbell rang.

"Who is it?" she asked from the couch.

"It's me," Sheena said on the other end.

Melodee got up immediately and headed for the door. "I was just about to call you," she said as she balanced herself on the balls of her feet to look through the peephole.

She closed one eye and used the other to look through the tiny glass hole in her door. Her eyes widened and she gasped, stepping back from the door while cupping her mouth. Instead of seeing Sheena's face, she saw a printout from an online gossip magazine pushed up against the peephole. The first thing Melodee noticed was a photo of she and Amir sitting in the booth at the Pelican Grill, smiling, with his arm draped over her shoulder.

Melodee swallowed hard as she unlocked the door. And when she opened it, Sheena stood on the other side with her lips tight and eyes narrowed. She stared at Melodee with a look that had the power to turn Melodee into a pillar of salt.

In Sheena's hand, she clutched the printout.

Without saying a word, she pushed past Melodee and walked through the condo's door turning around to face Melodee once inside.

"Guess Who's Off The Market?" she said, reading the headline of the article. "R&B heartthrob and People Magazine's pick for Sexiest Man Alive last November, Amir Jones, is now a taken man. This photo was snapped by one of our inside sources close to the singer while he and his new lady dined out in Montego Bay's Pelican Grill in Jamaica following Amir Jones and platinum-selling rapper, Abacus', final show..." She glared up at Melodee. "On Friday."

Melodee blinked twice. "Sheena—"

"According to our inside source," Sheena continued reading, "Amir Jones and his mystery woman cuddled in a private nook of the restaurant and could not take their eyes or hands off one another," Sheena's nostrils were flaring when she gave Melodee a cold hard stare. "So, that's why I couldn't get in touch with your sneaky ass this weekend."

Sheena balled up the printout and hurled the paper ball at Melodee.

Melodee's heart was racing as she folded her lips into her mouth.

Sheena shook her head then looked Melodee up and down, disgusted.

"I wanted to tell you—"

"You wanted to tell me, what? That you're fucking my ex?"

"Sheena..."

"No," Sheena ordered. "You don't get to say shit right now."

Sheena paced back and forth "Aren't you curious how I found out? I was browsing through my Facebook feed while in line in the middle of a blizzard at the pharmacy to pick up yet another fucking ovulation kit. The irony, right? You're messing with the guy who put me in the situation that would have me buying what feels like my 100th ovulation kit. Do you understand how fucked up that made me feel?" Tears pooled in her eyes when she said, "I cried my eyes out to you just the other day."

"You did, and I'm sorry for—"

"I'm. Not. Done!" Sheena yelled, her voice echoing around the condo. "You know what's fucked up, Melodee? Not you fucking my ex-boyfriend, who you were aware was also my first love. Although, yes, that part is fucked up, but what hurts the most is that you kept it from me. We're supposed to be like sisters. We tell each other everything...or told each other everything. You already knew I blamed him for the shit I'm going through now with trying to conceive and the role he played in that and you still messed with him. You shouldn't have even gotten that close to him to get to this point."

Melodee dropped her head disappointed in herself. "I'm so sorry."

Sheena looked at her with tears in her eyes and said, "Oh, you're sorry… that's original. I can't do shit with your sorry, Melodee. Will your sorry help me give my husband a baby? Will it?!"

A tear fell from Melodee's eye and slipped down the curve of her cheek.

"You fucked him at his party that night, didn't you?"

Melodee shook her head. "No. It didn't happen that night."

"Oh... so you went back for the dick?" Sheena asked shaking her head.

"It wasn't like that, Sheena."

"What was it like? You didn't want him back in high school but now he's got all this money it's all good now?"

Melodee looked at Sheena with wrinkled brows. "You know I'm not like that."

"I thought I knew what you were like and who you were but now I have no fucking idea. I suspected the two of you messed around in high school when he and I were together so I wasn't too surprised to learn about this. Y'all were always too close for my comfort. It didn't matter though because I trusted you. Silly me."

"We never did that until recently."

"Hmph, and I should believe you, huh? Melodee's so damn honest and tells me everything, right?!"

They stood there silent, and so far apart from each other, the nose of Amir's chartered private plane could fit between them.

Sheena sniffed back the tears that were forming in her eyes and wiped away the ones that had already fallen. "You're lucky I got so much love for you. Had this been anybody else, I would've wiped the floor with their ass in their own house."

Melodee sighed as she looked away.

"I'm out of here," Sheena announced.

When she brushed past Melodee, Melodee tried to grab her arm to get her friend to stay longer so they could talk, but Sheena pulled her arm away.

"Don't touch me, bitch," she sneered. "Don't call me either. Don't even think about me."

Sheena opened Melodee's door and stepped out into the hallway. "In fact, forget I even exist. We," Sheena said pointing at herself and back at Melodee, "are no longer cool. Go have fun with your secret lover. I hope he was worth ruining 13-years of friendship."

Chapter Fourteen

Piles of shoveled snow sat on the side of the road on sidewalks, causing people to hop and jump when crossing by the crosswalk. The air was cold and the sky darker than usual for 6 p.m. Melodee drove through the city in her white Audi on her way to Amir's loft with tears in her eyes, her chest holding a heavy heart. There was a sticky heat forming in the back of her neck, a mix of nerves and guilt. She felt horrible knowing that she'd hurt Sheena. The one person who had been there for her when she needed someone the most. The time she spent with Amir that she believed to be like a dream, now left her dealing with a nightmare. To sneak behind Sheena's back and leave the country without saying a word. This was not like her. Melodee was embarrassed and decided an hour after Sheena left to drive to Amir's loft to tell him she couldn't be with him anymore.

Her relationship with Sheena was more important, she believed. She needed to fix that friendship before it was too late. She pulled up to the side of Amir's loft in front of a fire hydrant. Parking was damn near impossible to secure in the city at that hour so she figured she'd risk getting the ticket.

The doorman didn't even phone up Amir to inform him Melodee had arrived. He let her go upstairs having recognized her. Unbeknown to Melodee her face and now her name was slowly becoming recognizable across the urban market. It took that one article posted on the online magazine to be shared 1.2 million times on social media, sourced on blogs and other websites, and mentioned as blurbs on entertainment news channels. News traveled fast, especially when that juicy news involved Amir.

When she knocked on the door, Amir opened it. He was shirtless wearing just a pair of jogging shorts. His eyes stretched with surprise to see her.

"Hey Mel," he said leaning forward to kiss her on her cheek. "What are you doing here?"

He was so excited to see her that he hadn't noticed her eyes that were turning red from her crying.

"I wasn't expecting to see you until tomorrow," he continued pulling her into the loft by her hand and escorting her up to his bedroom."

"A.J…"

"Remember that special thing I said I wanted to show you?" he asked. He was smiling big and holding her hand tight.

In the background, he played Al Green's "How Do You Mend A Broken Heart." The fuzzy scratching as the record spun on the turntable beneath its needle gave hint that he wasn't playing a CD, but a vinyl record, most likely one given to him by his father.

They got up to his room and there were racks of dresses, different from the night of his club appearance. On his bed were four sequined gowns: one white, two gold, and another gold and white. All of them shimmered under the light and were extravagant and gorgeous.

"Denise made a few calls while in Jamaica. She figured I'd want you to be my date at the Grammys. You won't believe how many designers want to dress you, Mel!"

"A.J.—"

"I apologize about that leaked photo. I'm sure you've heard the news already. I'm not sure who that inside source was... gonna find out, though. But I'm not mad everybody knows either," he said walking up to her and pulling her close to him, "I want the whole world to know about us."

He realized she wasn't saying much and finally got an opportunity to look at her. That's when he saw the frown pulling her lips down and the dark circles forming beneath her eyes from her crying.

"What's the matter?" he asked, holding her face in his hands.

Melodee dropped the weight of her head into his palms. "I can't go to the Grammys with you.

"What?"

"I can't be with you. We can't do this anymore."

Amir looked at her confused. He shook his head and folded his lips into his mouth and was quiet for a moment.

Amir asked, “why not?"

Melodee sighed heavy. "Sheena knows about us."

Amir shrugged. "Okay, and?"

"She's my best friend."

"Not this shit again," he murmured. "So, what that got to do with you being with me?"

"She was your girlfriend, A.J."

Amir threw his hands in the air and said, "In fucking high school!" His voice was so loud it startled Melodee. Noticing his tone was off, he took a deep breath to calm himself. "We dated in high school, that was twelve years ago, why can't we move past that?"

"You got her pregnant."

Melodee's lips trembled and tears fell from her eyes.

He walked up to her. "Mel, please don't cry." He placed his hands on her cheeks again while looking in her eyes and added, "Don't do this to us."

"I don’t have much of a choice."

"Of course you do."

They were both silent.

"I don't fucking get it!" he yelled in frustration pulling away. "You love me and I love you. Me and your friend dated in high school but things didn't work out. Why are you letting that affect us?"

"She can't have a baby because of you," Melodee blurted. As the words left her lips, they fell on Amir's ears like jagged boulders. Everything around them went deaf. The music playing in the background, the soft mist of the diffuser on his dresser dispersing essential oils into the air. Nothing else could be heard. Her words laid on the floor like a loaded grenade. The room was eerily quiet.

"What did you say?" he questioned.

Melodee walked up to his bedroom wall and pressed her back against it, leaning her head back. "When she had her abortion senior year, they dilated her cervix too much. Her doctor told her, after she had a miscarriage a month before her wedding, that her cervix may have been too tight and when they dilated it enough to abort the baby, the tissue was weakened in the process," she sighed and took a breath. "This is the reason it's been difficult for her to conceive or carry a baby past the first trimester. She can't have a baby and she blames you for that."

The tears fell before she could stop them. Amir stood in front of her still, motionless, staring back at her in disbelief.

"I haven't a single clue why she wants a baby, but she does," Melodee added. "She wants the stress, the staying up all night trying to figure out what a crying baby wants. She wants the shitty diapers, the spit up on her favorite t-shirt. Sheena wants all that. But she can't. She hates me now. My best friend hates me because I'm involved with you."

"Mel, listen to me—"

"And I love Sheena too much to hurt her like this."

"Mel," Amir tried to interject again. He was in front of her with her face in his hands trying to get her to meet her eyes with his, but she wouldn't.

"It seems like these babies who don't even exist yet just keep fucking up my life. Jaden left me because I didn't want to have a baby and Sheena's mad at me because she wants a baby she can't have. I can't win."

Amir lifted her chin. "Mel, please look at me."

When she finally did, her heart felt like it broke into a thousand pieces inside of her chest.

"We can make this work."

Melodee closed her eyes and shook her head. "No, we can't."

"You want me to call her to apologize and explain everything? I will. I'll do whatever you want me to do, Mel, just please don't do this," he pleaded.

She watched tears pool in his eyes and how he took deep breaths to keep them from falling. Her heart grew weak in her chest as she pressed her palm against the wall to push herself off it.

Melodee looked down at the dresses on the bed then back at him. "This lifestyle might be too much for me, anyway. Seeing my picture in anything besides a picture frame is strange, it makes me uncomfortable. And the women—"

"You'll get used to it," he insisted. "And if you don't, I'll give it all up. I don't need this, any of this. But I need you, Mel."

"Music is who you are, A.J."

"No, it's not. It's what I do. My mama dying proved that none of this shit really matters."

He hung his head and Melodee reached out to him noticing his pain.

"You know why I called nobody including you for my mama's funeral? I didn't know who I could trust. I wasn't sure who would be the asshole to send my mama's photo of her in a coffin to the highest bidder. People were calling me asking for a ticket to her funeral. A fucking ticket! Like it was an event. So, I kept it private. I wanted you to be there, I wanted your parents there, too. Mama would've wanted all of y'all to be there, but I hadn't spoken to you in so long... I didn't know who to trust."

Melodee wiped the tear that was falling from his eye.

"Besides Ant, you're the only person I can trust now, Mel. The only person I can depend on to keep it real with me and love me for me and not because I'm Amir Jones. You don't even call me Amir. Something so simple like the name you call me holds so much meaning to me. I feel good when you're around and like my old self when I'm with you."

Melodee let out an uneven sigh. His words stirred in her mind as she weighed her options. Their time together had been more than a physical thing. It was clearly love. But the look in Sheena's eyes, her being so hurt, flashed through her mind like red strobe lights. The words Sheena said to Melodee, the shock of betrayal that pierced through Melodee's heart like a serrated blade. She couldn't deal with the idea of betraying her friend. It didn't sit right with her. Melodee shook her head slow. "We can't do this anymore, A.J., I'm sorry," she said, her eyes avoiding eye contact with Amir's.

He pressed his forehead against hers. "You can't even look at me when you say that. You don't want this."

Melodee got choked up, and she struggled to find the words to say, but speaking any more words would make the situation harder than it already was. "I gotta go."

"Mel, please, I love you."

The tears fell from both of their eyes as Melodee pulled away and quickly walked down his glass staircase. Hot tears were pouring down her face when he yelled her name from the top of the stairs.

"Mel," he called down to her again. She kept walking, running now toward his door.

"Melodee, I need you," was the last thing she heard him say before she slid the front door closed behind herself.

She stood in front of the door for a moment, pressing her back against it and muffling her cries by clasping her hands over her mouth. After a few seconds, her hand was on the knob knowing that all she needed to do was slide it back open, run back into Amir's arms, and they'd just continue their love affair.

But Sheena was hurt. And on the scale of what mattered the most, love or loyalty, loyalty had never failed Melodee while love left her broken not long ago.

Down in her car, with an orange ticket tucked beneath her windshield wiper, she cried into her steering wheel. She only drove off when she glimpsed Amir pushing open the lobby's glass door and running out in search of her.

Chapter Fifteen

It was five minutes to 5 p.m. Melodee knew this because she hadn't stopped glancing down at her watch since returning from lunch. She'd been able to put thoughts of Amir out of her mind. That was until that morning when she couldn't escape the sound of his voice. He'd released his album with no warning during the early morning hours and the streets were going insane. As Melodee made her way to work that morning and during her lunch break, songs from Amir's album played from car speakers, loudly through headphones plugged into people's ears on the train, and on the radio in the deli she bought her sandwich. The only place not playing his album was in Dr. Sherida Pierce's office, and it probably would have been if Sherida had gotten the chance to buy the album before coming into work.

Soft elevator music played throughout the office instead as Melodee counted down the time left before her shift ended. It had been a week since she last spoke to Amir and Sheena. She'd been calling Sheena since the day Sheena confronted her. Melodee wanted to tell Sheena that her relationship with Amir was over and how she was sorry. But Sheena wouldn't take her calls.

Every time she called Sheena's home, her husband Ray answered the phone. Judging by the shakiness in his voice when he'd tell her Sheena wasn't home, Melodee sensed Sheena was right there telling Ray to say that. While Melodee was calling Sheena, Amir was calling Melodee. He'd been blowing up her phone since the night she ran out of his loft. That night, she saw him come down as she cried in her car. Before he could see her, she started her car up and barreled down the street away from him.

At night, sleep was impossible. Melodee had watched daybreak every morning for the past week and not because she wanted to see the sunrise. She hadn't smiled in days and her heart felt empty, again.

While her personal life was taking a hard hit, her work life had improved. All it took was Sherida seeing Melodee slide into a million-dollar car for Sherida to change her perspective and attitude toward her receptionist. That and Sherida seeing the infamous photo of Amir and Melodee sitting super close in that Montego Bay restaurant. Since returning to work that Monday, Sherida had been sweet as pie toward Melodee. Smiling ear-to-ear whenever she spoke with Melodee, not being a phone Nazi the moment it rang. In fact, she discarded her no personal calls rule entirely, especially considering that one of those personal calls could be from Amir Jones.

Sherida poked her head outside of her office when Melodee pushed her chair back to stand up from her desk. "Heading out now?" Sherida asked.

Melodee pulled air through her nose and forced herself not to roll her eyes at Sherida's brand new stage-five clingy behavior. Melodee couldn't so much as cross her legs in the office without Sherida happily inquiring about what she was doing. Sherida had been waiting patiently for Melodee's desk phone to ring and it be the R&B heartthrob, of whom she owned every album he'd ever released, calling. Melodee couldn't bring herself to tell Sherida that her relationship with Amir wasn't a relationship anymore. Besides, Melodee would take Sherida's new attitude over her old one. The charade would have to continue.

"Yup," Melodee replied pointing at her laptop and adding, "I've set up your calendar for tomorrow. All of your appointments have been confirmed."

"No calls today for you?" Sherida asked with a bright smile, ignoring Melodee's work talk.

Melodee forced her lips to pull into a smile. "Nope. He's a busy man," she lied. "He did just release an album."

"I know! I'm going to go pick it up right after leaving from here." Sherida rubbed her palms together then said, "Maybe he can call tomorrow?"

Melodee shut her eyes tight, trying her best to maintain her smile. "Maybe."

Melodee couldn't get on that elevator and down to the lobby fast enough. As she waited for the elevator to make it to their floor, she pressed on the call button as if doing so would make the elevator get to her sooner.

As she passed by security, one of Amir's songs off his new album played from the small radio on the security guard's desk.

"Your boy's album is bananas! Every single song is fire," the heavyset guard bragged to Melodee. He like everyone else close to her knew they were together.

Melodee smiled politely and nodded her head.

She hadn't listened to the album yet. Not because she had any ill feelings toward Amir. She felt listening to him in any way through music or talking would make her miss him even more than she already did.

The minute Melodee stepped out the doors of the office building and into the bitter New York cold, she scrolled through podcasts like she always did after leaving work. She stopped on one of her favorite podcasters, Lamar at Knight, two guys who recorded their podcast at the XM Sirius radio station near Rockefeller Center.

But she didn't stop on their podcast because of that. In the description, she read that the guest for the evening was Amir.

She didn't hesitate to click into the station. And when she did his rendition of "Simply Beautiful" was playing.

The tears flooded her eyes, immediately. Now knowing that his decision to record and add the song to his album was influenced by her made the song even more sentimental for her.

She ducked into Bryant Park just a few blocks away from the office. It was fairly empty since there were piles of snow everywhere which was why she chose there to sit. Melodee didn't want to draw any attention with her tears as she listened with her ears plugged.

"That was one of the songs that appears on Amir Jones' spanking new album, Black Rose, in stores as of this morning," radio host Lamar said through Melodee's headphones. "We got the man of the hour in the studio, right now."

"Yes, I am, what up y'all!" Amir said.

"You dropped a bomb on us this morning by releasing this album unexpectedly. Was that the plan?" the other host, Knight inquired.

"Kind of," Amir replied, "I wanted to release the album when it was ready instead of announcing a release date then pushing it back because it wasn't done. Or worse rushing the process just to get it out there because I promised to do so by a certain date. So, I went rogue with it."

"How'd your label react to that?" Lamar asked.

"Oh, they hated the idea with a passion when I suggested it to them last week. They thought I got my hands on some bad weed."

They all laughed and Melodee snorted to herself.

"But I told them I'd take full responsibility whether it tanked or did well. Plus, I wanted to see if I had the same clout as Beyoncé." Amir laughed.

"Well apparently you do because you've already sold seven hundred thousand copies in fifteen hours and experts are projecting your sales for a million in the next four days. You'll probably double that by next week," Lamar announced. "In today's music climate, that's beyond major."

The sound of clapping echoed throughout the studio.

"Sounds good to me," Amir said.

"It's been an incredible few months for you," Lamar continued. "You just wrapped up one of the hottest joint tours in years. You're getting ready to hit up the Grammys where you're nominated for eight awards, you were named People's Sexiest Man Alive three months ago—"

"Super dope, by the way. Representing for the brothers," Knight added.

"No doubt," Amir replied.

"And... you got yourself a new lady."

Amir laughed and Melodee could sense a slight undertone of discomfort in his voice.

"The photos are everywhere of the two of you in Jamaica."

"Yes, I see that," Amir said.

"Care to share a little about her?"

There was silence.

"Uh-oh ladies, he's smiling real big," Knight revealed.

"I won't say too much," Amir said. "All y'all need to know is she's someone special."

"Shh, you hear that, Amir?" Lamar quizzed.

"What?"

"The sound of hearts breaking across the world because of what you just said."

Everyone laughed in the studio.

"They crying over you, Mr. Jones. You do know that most of your fans are women, right?"

"Well aware," Amir insisted. "And I love all my fans very much. But this woman, I love even more."

A smile spread across Melodee's lips.

"Is she an up-and-coming artist or something? Everyone is dying to know how you two met," Lamar said.

"Nah, she's not in the business. We went to high school together. She was one of my really close friends... and I used to date her best friend."

"Whoa!" Knight said.

"Yeah, that's too much of a long story and way too private to talk about."

"I'm more surprised that they had girls looking as fine as your lady in high school. What high school was that?"

There was laughter in the studio.

"I'd never miss a day of school. And I probably would've never graduated looking at girls like her," Lamar joked.

"Aye, don't look too hard," Amir warned before bursting into laughter. "Anyway, my mama used to adore her. She always told me she liked her. This woman is a real genuine person and very loyal. She's someone whose got my heart.

"So, are you taking her to the Grammys this year?" Knight inquired.

Amir was quiet for a moment. He cleared his throat then said in the best upbeat voice he could muster up, "that's the plan."

Melodee unplugged her ears. The air was getting colder around her when she blew into her hands to warm them up before slipping on her gloves. In her lap, she could still make out Amir's voice as he continued to whisper through her headphones. Hearing his voice warmed her right up, the heat radiating through her chest. It also warmed her spirit knowing he was still optimistic about their relationship. And when she wanted to give into the urge to call him, Sheena's angered face popping up in her mind stopped her. So, she called Sheena instead. But there was no answer, the call went straight to voicemail.

Later that week, on a Sunday, dressed in her NYU school pullover and a pair of black leggings, Melodee curled up on her couch with a glass of red wine prepared to relax before having to head into the office on Monday.

Her email was blowing up with interview requests, magazine features, and the like. She wondered how these people found her email address and considered blocking a few.

And her popularity via social media had skyrocketed. Melodee had over 10K friend requests on Facebook and close to 100K follow requests on Instagram. She'd stop watching TV because her name had come up one too many times when she tuned into an entertainment news channel to shamelessly catch up on Amir news since she wasn't speaking to him.

She'd finally worked up enough courage to download his new album days after it had been released. After listening to just a few songs played from other people's stereos and feeling her heart ache in her chest, she thought listening to Amir's whole album alone, would be too much. But that Sunday, she downloaded his album and listened to it via her laptop. Playing Black Rose from the first track to it's last, keeping it on heavy rotation.

She was listening to it for the third time that day. There was no denying it - The hype was justified. Black Rose was phenomenal, his best body of work yet. As his fourth studio album, Black Rose would cement Amir as one of the greatest artist in R&B.

Melodee swayed from left to right on her couch to his songs, each one connecting to her in a different way. She could say gratefully that she was one of the lucky few who got to listen to some of the songs off the now hit album before anyone else. The only person to make love to it before anyone could think to do it after its release.

Every time his version of "Simply Beautiful" started up, her heart would beat a little faster and she'd shut her eyes tighter. She was lost in the sound of Amir's voice when her cellphone vibrated on her coffee table.

"Hey, Melodee," Big Ant said on the other end of her phone when she answered.

"Ant? Hey, what's up?"

"Are you busy right now? I was wondering if I could stop by your place for a quick visit."

Melodee glanced at the time. It was 10 p.m. and usually when she liked to head off to bed.

Noticing her silence, he added, "I won't be too long, I promise. I'm right downstairs, anyway"

"What?" she replied walking over to her window and peering down at Big Ant's black Range Rover parked across the street. "And how did you find out where I lived, man?"

He chuckled. "Amir's driver told me. So, are you gonna let me come up or nah?"

Big Ant's eyes were all over Melodee's condo the moment he stepped through the door.

"Excuse me, college girl," he said, his eyes still scanning. Her fireplace mantel that once held pictures of she and her ex-husband, Jaden, was now bare but still beautiful. She had the fire blazing over coal in the fireplace to keep the place warm and it cast a somber orange glow around the living room. "How can you afford this place on a receptionist income, again? You working for Dr. Phil or something?"

Melodee giggled. "The ex-husband gave it to me after the divorce."

"Not bad," he said walking over to her couch. "May I?" he asked pointing down at her couch asking for permission to sit.

“Of course," she said. "Can I get you anything to drink?"

"No, I'm okay. I just wanted to stop by to talk to you about, A."

Melodee was in the kitchen pouring herself another glass of wine when she sighed into her throat. "That doesn't surprise me."

"He told me what happened."

Melodee looked over at Big Ant who stared back with his full brown eyes. His eyes were as round as the rest of him.

"He *just* told you?"

"Well, he told me you wouldn't be coming around as much anymore last week. But he told me why after his radio interview. I've had to talk him out of coming here a few times. I told him to give you some space to think things through. So, I figured I'd stop by to help you think those things through." He smiled

Melodee nodded. "And you're here to tell me to—"

"Reconsider," Big Ant suggested.

Melodee shook her head.

"Hear me out, now," Big Ant pleaded, throwing his hands up in mock surrender.

She nodded, giving him her approval to continue.

"Before he spotted you by the bar from his VIP box in Club Déjà Vu, Amir was just... existing."

"What do you mean?"

"Not present, kind of like on autopilot," Big Ant clarified. "Ms. Anita dying on the first of January, the first day of the year, left him spinning. No sense of direction, no care for anything. He had nothing to look forward to. But all that changed that night y'all ran into each other. Before Club Déjà Vu, he hadn't so much as smiled unless he needed to do it."

Melodee looked at him with wrinkled brows.

"I mean, he'd smile for pictures, he'd smile during his TV appearances but he wasn't smiling from the heart. I'm talking about a smile so real it makes your cheeks hurt. A smile you can see without seeing it, just from looking at the person's eyes. He hadn't done that since his mama died and did it again with you."

He scooted to the front of her couch to thumb through her opened psychology textbook on her coffee table. His right brow rose, impressed. "He admires your mind, Melodee, something he doesn't do with these other women who waste his time. And because you two were already friends—"

"Ant, the situation is too damn complicated."

"I'm aware." Big Ant nodded. "He told me all about Sheena and her trouble conceiving."

Melodee nodded.

"See, I can relate to her struggle. Shanice and I had a hard time trying to get pregnant. We tried everything besides In vitro, so I get how difficult trying to conceive can be."

"And you know Sheena can't carry a baby because Amir forced her to have that abortion, right?"

"He told me."

"So, then you understand my dilemma. It's not only that she's my best friend, and they used to date. It's that the one reason she can't move on is because of a decision she made in the past that is affecting her future in a major way."

"I know."

"She hates me, Ant. Like the, if-I-could-kill-you-by-just-looking-at-you-I-would, kind of hate. She won't take my calls. She's got her husband lying about her not being home no matter what time I call. I feel horrible, disloyal, and like the worse friend ever. I shouldn't have done that to her for how good she's been to me."

Big Ant ran his palms from his thighs to his knees. "I know better than anyone else how strong your bond with Sheena is. Mine is the same with A, so I get it. But sometimes, you're gonna do some things your best friend is gonna hate you for doing."

"It can't be this though. I can't be with him if she truly believes he ruined her life. A.J. will be fine without me, he's got plenty of options from what I can see." Melodee picked up her wine glass and took a sip of her wine.

Big Ant let out a heavy sigh. He was silent before saying, "I don't need to be here with you every day to understand all the attention you've been getting as of late has been getting on your last nerve, am I right?"

Melodee let out a breathy exhale and nodded her head. "It's been crazy."

"Well, imagine having to deal with that every day for close to ten years. And on top of that - harsh criticism, unrealistic expectations, pressure to be better than your last accomplishment, all the while being surrounded by phony ass people who will tell you anything they think you want them to say so they can stay on your good side."

Big Ant stood to his feet to join Melodee by her kitchen. "With his mama being gone, the number of genuine people he has in his corner is close to none. Besides me, he got no one else he can really trust to keep it real with him. His own family can't be trusted." He paused before continuing. "I keep him grounded and Ms. Anita used to, too. But now I'm married and about to be a daddy."

Melodee gasped, then pressed her hand to her chest. "Oh my God, Anthony, congratulations!"

He smiled. "Thank you." He placed one hand on her shoulder and continued. "So now that my time will be spent with him even less, that leaves him exposed to all types of shit. Melodee, I'm surprised the brother is still only smoking weed having been in this business for the amount of time he's been rocking with music. The parties he attends, the people he's around, if not careful he can get sucked in, in the worse way."

Melodee sighed.

"Now, I'm not saying for you to be a babysitter. Far from that. I just see that you two love each other, like really love each other. He makes you smile and you do the same for him. When y'all look at each other, it's like no one else exists. It's some trippy shit to witness but hey, it's y'all thing."

They both laughed.

"He's in love with you, Melodee."

Melodee looked at him, her eyes tearing.

"For real, for real."

Big Ant walked along the hardwood floor, the wooden planks creaking beneath his feet, as he stepped toward her window to glance down at his car.

He turned back to face her. "To keep it real with you, I'm not even used to these kinds of visits. I'm usually banging down a groupie's door to either take back something she stole from his place or ordering her to delete private photos of him off her social media account. This right here, standing in a woman's living room asking her to take him back because he's in love with her... this is some new shit for me."

Melodee tried to fight back her smile as she sat down on the stool at her kitchen's island.

"All I'm asking is for you to think about it. I know Sheena is your friend and if I could put myself in her shoes, I know I'd be pissed as hell if A started talking to my ex. But he ain't no random guy to you. Your relationship with him is so different. The two of you have been friends for a real long time and clearly the gap in time that you hadn't talked didn't matter at all because y'all picked right back up where y'all left off at." He smirked. "Including your mutual enjoyment of Mary Jane's company."

Melodee laughed.

"He ever tell you why he didn't invite you to Ms. Anita's funeral?"

Melodee nodded. "He wasn't sure who to trust."

"Yup. They tried to turn that woman's funeral into a circus. Phones were getting confiscated by the minute because family members couldn't help themselves, snapping photos of her in her coffin with plans to sell them to websites and magazines. We couldn't hear the final prayer as they lowered her body into the ground because someone leaked the burial location to the media. Paparazzi helicopters showed up, circling overhead at her gravesite."

"Damn," Melodee whispered.

"It was a fucking mess," Big Ant added. "But I say all of that just to show you how much Amir needs us."

A tear fell from her eye.

"This business, the entertainment world, can be a cold ass bitch. She'll lure you in, fuck you, then spit you out when she's taken all your worth. With you by his side, future doctor." He beamed. "My boy, A, will be at his best. That's why Ms. Anita always wanted you for him from the very beginning."

"What are you talking about?" Melodee asked.

Big Ant let a kid-like smile crease the sides of his lips. "I'll leave you with that." He walked over to her, pulled her into a bear hug then headed to her front door, pulling it open.

Before closing it behind himself he said, "Just think about calling him, Melodee. Despite what you might think, he'll never be fine without you."

Chapter Sixteen

The minutes became hours, and the hours became days that Big Ant's words stirred in Melodee's mind like a funnel of air disorganizing her thoughts. Every night since their talk, she'd come home from work, pick up then put down her phone, wanting to call Amir but deciding against dialing his number. It was now going on two weeks since they last spoke or saw each other and his interview paired with Big Ant's visit left her questioning her decision to end things.

But it's the right thing to do, she'd tell herself when tears watered her eyes. Just hearing his voice filled her empty heart a little, and the only way she could listen to his voice but keep him away was to repeatedly replay his album. Melodee listened to Black Rose everywhere. In the shower while getting ready for work, on the train, during her breaks, and as she returned from work and got ready for bed. Amir stayed on her mind and in her ears. To her this was the closest thing to being with him.

That night, she played his album for what would seem like the 100th time when the buzz of her intercom system interrupted her jam session. She glanced at the time. It was after 9:30 p.m.

"It's Sheena, Melodee," Melodee heard after asking who it was. She paused in shock in front of her boxed intercom, her finger still on the listening button.

"We need to talk," Sheena continued, figuring her pop-up visit surprised Melodee. So, Melodee buzzed her in and waited for the knock at her door.

When she pulled open the door, she and Sheena locked eyes for the first time in weeks. Melodee examined Sheena's expression. Sheena managed a half-smile and Melodee determined Sheena wasn't there for blood.

"Should I hide my knives before letting you come into my home?" Melodee joked and Sheena laughed.

Melodee stepped aside and Sheena walked through the door. Like the night she showed up with the printout, Sheena turned on her soles and started to say something but Melodee spoke first.

"I'm really sorry, Sheena. I know saying sorry isn't enough but I want you to understand that I never wanted to hurt you."

"Melodee—"

"Hold on, let me finish. This is something I wanted to tell you but you haven't been taking my calls."

Sheena hung her head for a moment, looking back up at Melodee.

"You're my best friend," Melodee continued. "You've been there for me when I needed someone the most and I shouldn't have done that to you. That wasn't right."

"No, it wasn't," Sheena agreed. "Let's call it what it was, fucked up. But... I blew things way out of proportion."

Melodee's eyebrows squished together.

Sheena walked over to Melodee's couch, gesturing for Melodee to join her. Sheena ran her palms over her thighs and sighed. "I guess what made me angry was that I thought you were choosing Amir over me."

"What do you mean?" Melodee questioned.

"You didn't tell me about him and you, before or after something happened between y'all. Would I have accepted you and Amir being involved? Probably not. But I would have been less angry if you would've come and told me you had feelings for him, now, that were more than friendly. Fine, he and I aren't together anymore, haven't been for a very long time, but the fact that you kept a secret from me because of him... I thought our bond was stronger than that."

"Our bond is stronger," Melodee insisted, taking Sheena's hand. "My motivations for not telling you was not because I wanted to do dirt behind your back. I just didn't want to hurt you. Your situation with having trouble conceiving was too current. That mixed with A.J. being your ex-boyfriend and who you blame for that. I didn't want to break your heart."

Sheena looked Melodee in her eyes and asked, "do you love him?"

Melodee took a deep breath in and sighed. She shut her eyes and nodded her head.

Sheena arched a brow then smiled. "I always wondered why you hooked us up when you could have had him to yourself. Amir was one of the most if not the most handsome guy in our school. Every girl tried hard to get and keep his attention, including me even after I had him. With you though, it came so easy. He'd break dates with me to chill with you. I was never jealous of it though because you were my girl and you're loyal. I still always wondered why you never gave him a chance in high school. He wanted you."

Melodee shrugged. "I liked our relationship the way it was. It was laidback. I didn't have to worry if I had a hair out of place or if my breath smelled right. I could be silly and say stupid stuff without worrying if he'd like me after saying it. Our friendship was perfect, there was no pressure, and I didn't want to ruin that by involving emotions.

"Well, y'all are involved in more than emotions now," Sheena said, nudging Melodee with her shoulder. "I listened to his interview on that Lamar At Knight podcast the other day on a website. It's posted everywhere."

Melodee shook her head. "I ended things with him."

"Why'd you do that?"

"Because of you, duh."

"Well, that was dumb. He's clearly in love with you, from how he was talking."

Melodee fought but lost to the smile pulling at her lips. She fixed her lips when she realized what she was doing.

"Don't fight it now. You can smile about it," Sheena teased. "It's like I said, I wasn't mad you two hooked up... I thought y'all already did years ago. I was pissed you kept your relationship from me. We tell each other everything. Now that I know you were protecting me, I guess I won't kill you this time."

Melodee laughed and pulled Sheena into a hug. She let out an exhale and stood up, her feet pointing toward the kitchen. "So, red or white?" She asked referring to wine.

"Oh, none for me... that's the other reason I'm here."

Melodee turned to her.

"I'm pregnant!"

Melodee's jaw dropped. "What!"

"Yeah, 14-weeks."

Melodee's twisted her face. "Wait, what? How?"

"God, I guess." Sheena pressed her palms together and raised them over her head. "I went in for the appointment I skipped that day with you, and my doctor was feeling around my stomach and gave me a concerned look. She didn't want to say anything and both Ray and I were freaking out because the way she stared at us made us nervous. So, she brought in the ultrasound machine and did the same routine they do to check my ovaries."

"Okay," Melodee said, joining her back on the couch

"And there was a baby in there."

"I don't understand. Weren't you still getting your period?"

"Yeah, but you know my cycle is so irregular. My periods were shorter than usual, sometimes I would just be spotting, but I figured it was my body being funny again. But the doctor said some women still get their cycles until a certain point in their pregnancy. It's rare, but it happens."

"Wow, this is unbelievable. This whole time you've been walking around here pregnant?" Melodee leaned closer to Sheena and placed her palm on her stomach. "You're not even showing with your flat belly ass."

They both laughed.

"Had I went to the appointment that day with you, I would've known sooner." Tears gathered in Sheena's eyes and poured down her face. "I made it past the first trimester."

Melodee hugged Sheena, and they both cried together.

Sheena sniffed back her tears and wiped her eyes, Melodee doing the same.

"My doctor said the baby is healthy and everything looks good."

"That's amazing, I'm so happy for you," Melodee replied. "Now this explains why you've been eating so much. Busting down the olives at the club, eating my ice cream and yours at the ice cream shop."

"And those crab cakes at Coney Island," Sheena added, both of them laughing. She got serious when she said, "Listen, I'm not just saying this because things have changed for me. Maybe I am. Regardless, I want you to be happy, Melodee."

Melodee glanced down at her lap, eyeing her ring finger with the faint line of where her wedding band used to be.

"You and Amir were always meant to be, I see that now, and I don't want you to think you can't be with him because of me. Our thing was in high school. I'm married now and have moved on," Sheena insisted. "Maybe it was the hormones from this pregnancy that had me thinking crazy. But you're my girl, and I love you to the moon and back. If Amir can make you smile like how you were doing in Jamaica, then shit... he's the one."

Melodee smiled.

"You know what they say, one woman's trash is another woman's treasure," she teased.

"Shade?"

"I gotta shade you a little on this." Sheena giggled. "Seriously Melodee... the way he was talking about you in that interview and the way y'all look together, he's yours without a doubt. So, as your best friend I got to tell you," she said placing both her hands on each side of Melodee's cheeks, "you better go get your man, girl."

Chapter Seventeen

Melodee woke up the next day smiling before her eyes could see the sun. She glanced out of her window to see the clouds parting to make room for the sunlight to beam through her sheer white curtains. A burst of energy surged through her body as she stepped off her bed and dashed into her bathroom. After freshening up for the day, she threw on a pair of jeans, a sweater, Converses, and her down jacket.

She called her boss Sherida on her way to the hair salon to tell her she needed to take a personal day. When they spoke, Sherida was audibly annoyed, surely because this would mean she'd have to call up a temp agency to get a receptionist who wasn't familiar with the way she liked things done, to manage her day. She didn't put up a fight, though, only saying, "sure, enjoy your day off."

Melodee knew that had this been before it became news that she and Amir were an item, Sherida would have threatened unemployment. There's been over a dozen times Melodee has called Sherida requesting a day off so she could rest after pulling all-nighters studying in the school library the day before. And Sherida would give her hell for it. But Melodee didn't care that day because she had important plans for later that night.

She made the Friday a day of pampering and shopping.

She visited a salon to get her hair blown out, highlighted, and pin curled so she could keep it fresh looking when she took it down later that night. Melodee also stopped by a spa for a facial and massage before hitting up the Diamond District.

Handing the jeweler her pink diamond earrings for him to examine with his monoculars and quote her a price was as easy as melting ice. Her attachment to the pricey gift her ex-husband gave her on their wedding day was no longer there. She was pawning it, and using the cash to do something nice for a man she finally knew was meant for her, Amir.

From the Diamond District, she hit up 5th Ave & Madison to shop, but not for just anything. She stopped at the Burberry store and picked up the piece of clothing she knew for a fact Amir would love. She then moseyed over to the Manolo Blahnik store where she tried on and purchased a pair of pumps. La Perla was her last stop. There she purchased an all-black lace bra and panty set complete with garter and sheer tights.

After eating lunch inside of a small café, she was back at home around 5 p.m. She spent an hour in her bathtub under blue and pink water courtesy of her LUSH bath bomb. Her head lolled over her tub and her ears welcomed in the sweet sounds of Amir's voice for the umpteenth time. She caressed herself. And she anticipated seeing, as Sheena put it, her man, later that night.

Melodee's cab pulled away from the curb the moment she stepped out in front of Amir's loft. Her legs immediately felt the chill of the February winter air. If it weren't for the sheer stockings she wore, her legs would be like ice sticks. She squinted her eyes when she peered up at his window and saw the lights on. She smiled then hurried into the lobby.

The doorman's jaw practically hit the floor when she walked in all dolled up and pretty. But it was what she was wearing that damn near left him drooling.

Speechless, he motioned for her to go up, no sign in necessary as usual.

Melodee took a deep breath when the elevator reached the top floor. She hadn't spoken to Amir in almost two weeks and worried in that moment what his reaction would be. If he'd be happy to see her or just angry that she left him and hadn't been answering any of his phone calls when he said he loved and needed her.

She fought back that fear as she knocked on his front door. She could hear music playing and voices in the background before Big Ant unlocked then slid the loft door open.

He stared at her with widened eyes before letting them travel down the length of Melodee's body. He leaned his head to the side to glance around her and twirled his finger signaling for her to turn in place.

Melodee swatted that same hand.

He laughed. "Good lord woman, you about to make this man pass out at the sight of you."

She giggled. "Is he home?"

"Oh yeah, he's here. Been wandering around this place for the past few days in search of answers. He's been like a song without a melody. You see what I did there?"

"Such a poet."

Big Ant turned his chin over his shoulder and called for Amir but didn't get an answer.

"Can y'all keep it down for a moment, damn," Big Ant ordered to the ten people chatting and laughing in the loft. "Yo, A."

"Yeah?" he heard Amir yell back.

"You got something here at the door." Big Ant turned to check Melodee out again, and she placed her hand on her waist and used the other to snap her fingers in his face. "Excuse you, married man."

"Like I said, I'm married, but that has not affected my 20:20 vision. You got panties on under that?"

Melodee laughed.

"I don't want anything right now," Amir said back from inside of the loft.

"Trust me. You're gonna want this, brother," Big Ant insisted.

There were footsteps first before Amir said from behind Big Ant, "what is it?"

Big Ant stepped out of the way and Amir pulled the door open.

Amir's eyes widened the moment he saw it was Melodee, and he licked his lips when he realized what she was wearing.

It was a brown Burberry trench coat that stopped a few inches below her ample bottom and showed off the length of her legs.

The belt hugged her waist giving her bust a fuller look. Her blown out hair was smooth and thick, flowing down her back as she turned in place for Amir to get a better view of her. On her face was light foundation, blush, and a bold red lip just the way he liked it.

Amir's eyes had fallen to her feet when he sighed at the sight of her red pumps. It was the look he said he desired, down to the painted red lips, that night as he and Melodee chilled on the terrace.

"Everybody out," Amir demanded, to everyone inside the loft.

"What?" a few of his houseguests countered.

"I apologize, but y'all gotta go," he replied. With his eyes still on Melodee, he took her hand into his and kissed her on the back of her palm. "You're in trouble the minute I get you alone."

"What about the studio," a female said as she approached the door.

Before she could place her hand on his shoulder blade, Big Ant caught it midair. "Y'all heard the man. Get your shit and get out. Y'all need directions to the door? Bring your ass this way, please," Big Ant directed.

As Amir's houseguests filed out of the loft, they all looked Melodee up then down as they left. Most of the guests were women who looked a lot like the women at his after-after party that night he and Melodee first shared their kiss on his terrace.

"Who's that?" one woman asked as they walked past Amir and Melodee.

The other girl kissed her teeth then said, "Oh, that's his girlfriend."

Being referred to as his girlfriend made Melodee blush.

The loft was finally empty when Amir tried to pull Melodee close, but she gently resisted.

"I remember you telling me right there on that terrace that these women," she said, pointing toward the front door where everyone walked out of, "made it too easy for you."

"Too damn easy," he replied, unbuttoning his shirt as he walked behind her.

"Well, you won't have to worry about that with me because I'm gonna make you work for this, tonight."

"Is that right?" he asked following close behind her.

She nodded, pausing in front of him to ask, "You want my heels on or off?"

He sighed then stroked his chin, thinking. "On... for now."

A slow grin spread across her lips as he pulled his shirt off and unbuckled his dress pants.

"Leave those on... for now," she ordered.

Amir threw his hands up in mock surrender. He followed her up his glass staircase, watching as she climbed it, slowly placing one foot in front of the other.

"I've missed you so much, A.J.," she said when they were in his room.

"Not more than I've missed you," he replied.

She walked farther into his room, unknotting the belt of the Burberry trench coat. She turned around slow and allowed the coat to drop to the surrounding floor.

"Mmm, baby," he whispered beneath his breath as he got an eyeful of her La Perla lingerie.

"You still want me, right?" she quizzed.

"More than you know."

"Then I'm all yours," she said, flicking the light switch off, making the room dark. "But you gotta find me first."

He chuckled while moving slowly toward her. He bumped into the edge of his bed and it made a thud sound.

"Be careful," she teased. "I'll kiss it better if you find me in time."

Amir laughed, still moving toward her. "And when I find you, you know I'm never letting you go, right?"

There was a brief silence before Melodee asked, "You promise?"

The room lit up not a moment later when Amir found the switch and turned on the light. He was in front of her now, her back pressed against the wall. He stared into her eyes and fanned his fingers against her cheeks as he held her face in his hands. Their lips close, but not yet touching.

"I promise. With every part of me I give you my word, Mel."

Melodee raised her hand, folded all her fingers into her palm except for her pinky which she stuck out for him to take then asked, "pinky promise?"

He nodded and smiled that brilliant smile of his that made her heart skip beats, and he looped her pinky with his. She smiled back as he brought their pinkies to his lips to kiss.

"So, this is ironclad now, we pinky promised and everything," Amir joked. "This is real now, right? You and me?" Amir questioned.

Melodee pointed her eyes up and tapped her finger against her chin as she considered his question. When he kissed his teeth at her she giggled. "Yeah," Melodee confirmed. "You and me."

He used his finger to move her hair from her neck and kissed her in the space above her collar bone.

"Finally," he whispered on her neck. "I love you, you know that right?"

Her fingers clasped the back of his head as he pressed his body firm against hers. "And I love you."

Amir's hands moved like a magician, unsnapping her bra with one brisk move of his fingers. He removed it before slipping her panties and the sheer stockings she wore down over her hips. He unhooked the garter belts and dropped to his knees to move them all down over her knees like it was second nature. He showered her legs with kisses before hiking her right leg up over his shoulder so his tongue could leave wet circles between her thighs.

After a few minutes of Frenching her little pink nub, he smiled with pride, his lips still between her legs, when her muscles trembled on his lips. He carried her to the bed where she insisted she return the favor.

With her essence marinating on his tongue she invited him into her mouth, her lips forming a vacuum-like seal around the shaft of his dick. His hand was buried in her hair, her hand between her thighs. The moment more familiar to them than prior ones, their guards down, comfort with each other at its highest.

"Damn," he said, forming an O with his lips as she continued to go to work, "I got me a triple threat."

She released him when he pulled away. He scooped her up in his arms and walked her to the head of the bed. Amir pulled open his nightstand drawer and pulled out a condom, ripping the foil wrapper open with his teeth and smoothing the condom over his throbbing erection.

"She's beautiful," he said as he slid between her wet narrowed walls.

"Mmm," Melodee moaned, as she opened around him.

"She's smart," he added as he moved like a snake, gliding in and out, out then in. Slow and steady.

"Mmm-hmm," she moaned. Melodee's body came alive as she wrapped her legs around him and gripped his hips with her fingers, guiding him deeper into her with the heel of her foot.

"And... mmm, damn," he stammered, pausing to expel a breathless moan when the soft muscle inside of her squeezed him just the way he loved it. He pressed his palm against his headboard to get better leverage over her then added, "she gives amazing head."

Melodee licked her lips. Smoothing her fingers up his chest as he thrusted.

"I can finally agree that I'm blessed, now that I have you, baby."

The two rocked and swayed on the surface of the bed in response to each other's movements. Her heat enveloped him each time he penetrated her from every position he twisted her into. Melodee's body fell into a synchronized rhythm of clenching and releasing as Amir filled then withdrew himself between her thighs. He parted his lips to breathe air in then out like a marathon runner after turning over for her to mount him. She circled her hips on top of him and let her head hang back with closed eyes.

"Mmm, A.J. You feel so good," she moaned

They both were transported to a physical plane, in a trance like state in which thinking of anything else besides each other in that moment ceased to exist. Infatuation, love, lust, and excitement stirred in their bodies like a swirling wind tunnel. They were connected at the pelvis and lips, the acoustics of their bodies mending sounding off throughout the room. The sheets were tight in Melodee's hands when he pulled her to her knees. Their harsh breathing and muffled groans filling the room when Amir got back in rhythm. Whispers of *I love yous* were laced with so much lust it sounded erotic and a little sinful. Those three little words held more weight than gold as it left their lips and were uttered in hushed tones when they said it in each other's ears.

The act had gotten better with time, something Melodee didn't think was possible. They were enough for each other but couldn't get enough of one another, only stopping to change condoms.

At some point, it became a game for them to see who would tire out first or have the stronger orgasm.

"Mmm-hmm, there you go," he whispered when Melodee trembled beneath him as she came and her muscles quivered around him uncontrollably. "Keep coming, Mel. Keep coming for me, baby."

They took bets as they fought to catch their breaths as their bodies collided in their climatic exercise. Never taking a break and only returning to get back into their battle to make the other come faster.

Their love making alternated between being erotic to being playful. From being competitive to sensual again. They smiled at each other, muttered expletives when the pace felt too good, and laughed a little at each other after bellowing their moans from their final climax into the quiet space of the room.

When they'd had enough, Melodee collapsed in his arms, their bodies coiled into each other like always, as they fell asleep blissfully exhausted and looking forward to their tomorrow together.

Chapter Eighteen

The screams of adoring fans echoed outside the Staples Center as Melodee and Amir's black Bentley pulled up at the red carpet entrance of the 59th Annual Grammy Awards ceremony. Inside the car, Melodee's heart was beating a mile a minute, her palms sweating, and her foundation catching the sweat beads forming on her forehead. Through the tinted glass windows, she could see the setup of the red carpet - fans on the far right standing on an elevated platform, paparazzi below them behind red velvet ropes, and celebrities dressed in their best standing in front of the Grammy backdrop smiling for the flashing cameras.

The Los Angeles, California weather was very warm for February, but Melodee could still feel the breeze when she reached out for Amir's hand to take to step out of the Bentley. The moment the bottoms of her Chanel strappy sandals touched the asphalt of the floor outside of the Bentley, it was announced in overhead speakers that Amir had arrived.

Necks turned, fans screamed, and paparazzi glanced down at their cameras to make sure the source of their incomes had enough memory to get the shot of Amir and his new girl that every magazine in the country would pay top dollar to buy the next day.

The couple matched with their outfits that afternoon. Amir wore a white tux with gold accents, his white shirt underneath unbuttoned down to his chest. And Melodee was dressed in a sequined long white and gold gown with a deep v-neck in the front. The sparkling dress hugged her hips and stressed her hourglass figure. Her hair swept up into a high ponytail, makeup finished with a smoky eye and neutral brown lip.

He turned to her and took her hand, placing a kiss on her cheek. The crowd went wild. Noticing she was nervous by how she held his hand tight he said into her ear, "you're looking too good right now. Let's skip all of this and go back to the hotel."

Melodee laughed and said, "And miss all this?"

"You ready?" he asked.

Amir's team had been preparing Melodee for the past two days for her first red carpet event. Prepping her on how to answer questions if she were asked. How to stand to make sure all her pictures were flawless. It was stressful but exciting. In the car, Amir's publicist Denise reviewed key points regarding what to say and what not to say to reporters. She was adamant about Amir not confirming he and Melodee were a couple. He was only to say she was his date.

Amir nodded to the requests with no intentions of sticking to Denise's script.

Melodee took a deep breath and pushed the air through her lips, smiled then nodded.

As soon as she stepped out onto the carpet, paparazzi were calling Amir's name, competing for his attention.

"Over here, Amir Jones."

"*You look great, Mr. Jones."*

"Who are you wearing, Amir?"

When Denise motioned for Melodee to come to her so Amir could take photos alone, Amir held Melodee's hand tighter and shook his head at Denise, declining her suggestion.

"Melodee, over here," shouted another camera man.

Hearing her name called out, caught her off guard but made her smile.

"Beautiful," he shouted before a gang of other camera men vied for her attention, too.

It was time to do red carpet interviews, the one part that made Melodee nervous. She figured that Denise would insist that she come with her. Melodee hoped for that, but Amir wasn't having it. From one interviewer to the next, he kept Melodee by his side. Most if not all the questions were centered on Amir's newly released album, Black Rose.

Denise had done the job of fielding interviewers before the red carpet, knowing which ones would interview Amir. All except one. A popular blogger, Cassandra Rose, the only blogger allowed on the red carpet. The other bloggers were only allowed in the green room backstage at the award ceremony where the winners would be interviewed.

Cassandra motioned for Denise to come to her.

Denise squared her eyes at Cassandra, the lines around her eyes becoming more pronounced. She scratched her salt-and-pepper mane, hesitating, probably because Casandra was the blogger who purchased the photo of Amir and Melodee in Jamaica and posted it on her website for her millions of readers.

After Denise approached Cassandra and they had a brief exchange, Denise motioned for Amir and Melodee to walk over to speak with Cassandra next.

"I'm mad at you," was the first thing Amir said while wagging his finger at Cassandra. He was wearing a smile which gave hint he was only joking.

"I'm sorry," she said with a grin. "But I see you're here with the lady who had you smiling in Jamaica. Who are you two wearing?"

"Armani," Amir said for the millionth time on the red carpet. Every reporter asked the same thing in the same order. It was almost like déjà vu for Melodee.

"Nice! The two of you look amazing. So, first, congratulations on the three Grammys you've already won for Best R&B Performance, Best Urban Contemporary Album, and Best Rap/Sung Collaboration for your song with Abacus."

"Thank you." Amir grinned. "Just five more to go."

Amir glanced at Melodee and they smiled at each other.

Cassandra shifted her attention to Melodee then asked, "So how has newfound fame been for you, Melodee?"

Melodee chuckled. "Busy."

They all laughed.

"Matching outfits, holding hands, gazing into each other's eyes. Amir, everyone is dying to know... are you two a couple?"

Denise cleared her throat and tried to end the interview.

"It's okay," Amir said to Denise, who in response shook her head and insisted they go into the arena.

"No. Melodee's not my girlfriend," Amir said.

The reporters who were standing next to Cassandra, moved in closer, pushing their recorders and microphones in Cassandra's direction and toward Amir to be a part of the dialogue.

"She's my fiancé... if she says yes." He released Melodee's hand for the first time since arriving and motioned for Big Ant who was standing not far behind them. Big Ant pushed his hand into his suit jacket pocket and pulled out a small navy blue box.

"Oh my God," Melodee whispered.

Chapter Nineteen

Paparazzi nearly rushed the red carpet when Amir got down on one knee in front of Melodee with the small blue box in his hand.

The crowd went wild and foot traffic on the red carpet came to a complete stop. All eyes were on Amir and Melodee.

Melodee turned to Denise and Denise's jaw was slacked as she froze in place. But after Denise turned to see the hordes of fans screaming Amir's name, the celebrities clutching their chests in admiration, and the flashes of the cameras all over, she noticed how much good attention Amir and this move was getting. A smile so big you could see her gums and teeth creased her lips before she started prodding buttons on her Blackberry.

Melodee looked down at Amir on one knee in his white and gold tuxedo. He gripped the lid of the small box, preparing to lift it. Tears pooled in her eyes as her breathing got shallower.

"I told you I wanted to put something here," Amir said taking her hand into his and singling out her ring finger. Reporters with microphones and recorders leaned over the iron barricades as close as they could to capture every word he said. "And I'm a man of my word. I'm so ready to do this with you."

When he lifted the cover, inside spinning on a tiny turntable beneath a small light was an 11-carat natural pink diamond ring surrounded by a double row of round white diamonds set in platinum. Under the bright California sun, the ring glittered, winking like the flash from the paparazzi cameras. It was radiant cut and huge, protruding from the setting like it wasn't even a part of the ring.

Melodee brought her right hand to her mouth.

"Mel, the only thing bigger than this night is my love for you. It's always been you." He kissed the back of her hand. "I love you and want to be with you until my final breath. Love you in this lifetime and then again in the next. Can we seal this bond we have? Will you marry me?"

No one else mattered in that moment. The screams of the fans muted, the cameras stopped flashing, and all Melodee could see was Amir and his sparkling diamond ring. She tried to fight the thought but the pain of her divorce penetrated her mind in slow motion like a bullet moving through water.

Her lips trembled and a wave of goosebumps poked through the surface of her skin. She looked at her hand in his and the sincere look in his eyes that made her feel like it was just the two of them. He wasn't lying when he said he wanted to tell the whole world about them. Her future flashed before her eyes of a happier life with a man who truly loved her and supported her goals. She was in love with what she saw but more so in love with the man she'd share her vision with in real life. So, she took a deep breath and slowly let it out through her nose then parted her lips, showing all her thirty-two teeth.

"Yes," she replied with several head nods. "I'll marry you."

Celebrities with news that night would be pissed by the morning because all everyone will talk about is Amir proposing to his new fiancé, Melodee Delon, on the Grammy red carpet.

The crowd lost it, screaming his name and hers while jumping up and down in place. Melodee and Amir embraced each other with a hug and passionate kiss while the cameras sent off flashes with lightning quickness, zooming in to get shots of Melodee's ring.

None of that mattered to them. Amir and Melodee were in their own world. They kissed each other like they weren't on the red carpet of an event viewed by everyone and their mamas on Sunday night from their living rooms. When they finally came up for air, Denise ushered them off the carpet, the sound of reporters calling Amir and Melodee for comments could be heard behind their backs.

Inside, Big Ant kept story-hungry reporters back and turned away the few paparazzi who snuck past the back door of the venue to get exclusive photos of the newly engaged couple.

Melodee's heart raced and her head was light. She felt she was in a dream as her thoughts practically floated in her mind like a tag cloud.

Denise smiled big at Amir then stretched out her arms for a hug. "You are so damn hard-headed," she scolded. "But at least you know what you're doing. My phone has been blowing up since you got down on one knee. This wedding is going to be epic!"

"I told you being in love is a turn on for everyone, even the fans." He laughed.

Denise laughed and tapped him on his chest then turned to Melodee, lifting Melodee's left hand. Denise's dark brown eyes widened and she whistled at the sight of the pink diamond. "This ring and you are about to be so damn famous, honey." She smiled at Melodee then pulled her into a hug.

"Congratulations," Denise said, still embracing Melodee. "Welcome to Hollywood, Mrs. Jones!"

The End…*For now.*

Thank **YOU**

Dear Reader:

Thank you for reading Girl Code! Did you fall in love with Melodee and Amir like how I did? Creating these characters and this story was so much fun and I found myself loving how Melodee and Amir's relationship evolved organically.

They went from being friends to fiancées and it was a beautiful journey, but not without its bumps. But it's not over yet! While I was writing this novella, I had the idea to continue their story beyond Amir asking Melodee to marry him. So, there will be a spinoff of Girl Code, tentatively titled Mr. and Mrs. Jones. The story is already outlined and prepared to be written and will follow the couple from the aisle (their wedding and their honeymoon) through the first year of their marriage.

And through this new journey, there will be more than just bumps. Having any relationship survive in Hollywood is tough, throw in being married to one of the hottest R&B artists turned movie stars and you've got more problems than anxious groupies. Can't wait to get that one out to you. Make sure to join my BK Insiders Mailing list and to follow me via social media to stay in the loop of this follow up!

P.S. Let me know what you thought of Girl Code! Be a part of the convo, by using the #GirlCodeNovella hashtag via social media.

About Brookelyn Mosley

Brookelyn wrote her first short story when she was a sophomore in high school. Back then she discovered how using her experience as a teen living in Brooklyn to create romantic shorts was just as exciting to her as retail shopping and going on dates. After starting her first semester of college two years later, Brookelyn's creative writing became more of a hobby and something to do to escape the stress of midterms and finals. Now in her 30s as a freelance copywriter, penning short stories and novellas is her everything. While her experience with writing has evolved for the better, her undying love for creating fiction remains unchanged. Brookelyn's focus is on creating contemporary women's fiction with characters based in urban settings. Her stories chronicle the emotional journeys and erotic experiences of women today through her characters and the scenarios they're thrown into.

The motivation behind her brand of writing has a lot to do with what she discovered storytelling provided for her - an escape. Her goal with her work is to create characters and urban worlds that offer a great escape for fiction readers looking for a break from the daily grind of adulting and who prefer to relax with good books and short stories. When she's not freelancing, doing yoga, or showing her husband and toddler lots of love, she can be found sitting at her computer desk, with her legs folded, and a cup of coffee (or a glass of wine) at arm's reach as she types or edits her latest short or novella.

You can follow her on Twitter, Facebook, and Instagram under the handle @BrookelynMosley.

Email me at BrookelynMosley@gmail.com

Made in the USA
Middletown, DE
17 June 2021